Life's A Gamble

HEATHER MORRIS

ISBN: 1500951129
ISBN-13: 978-1500951122

THE COLVIN SERIES BOOK LIST
(SO FAR)

Book 1- Down to the Creek- Aiden & Karlie

Book 2- Nursery in Bloom- Austin & Leah

Book 3- Third Time's a Charm- Audrey & Maysen

Book 4- Life's a Gamble- Aaron & Amie

ACKNOWLEDGMENTS

To those who read my books and encourage me to get another one out there! Couldn't do it without your support!

1

"I'm sorry sir but you can't go back there, you'll have to take a seat in the waiting room." The nurse says to me at the clinic as soon as I get Audrey and Maysen there.

"I'm the one that brought them. I need to be in there for my little sister."

"No, she has requested that only her husband be in the room with her while she's having the baby. I'll come and update you as often as I can."

"Ok, thank you." I concede and walk to the waiting room. Mom and the rest of the family should be here soon. I drove a little too fast getting here and probably contributed to Audrey's anxiety. I feel a twinge of guilt as I realize that I should have thought of her instead of letting my wild side take over. Oh well, she's here safe and sound.

I sit in the nearest chair to the door and put my head in my hands. I hope this goes quickly. I need to get back home. Work on the airport starts next week and I have a ton of paperwork to get through beforehand. I knew I needed to be here for Austin's wedding but it sure isn't where I want to be. Audrey may need me now but I'm itching to leave again. This small town still isn't what I want or what I'm comfortable with. I don't know why out of all of my siblings I'm the one who can't stay in Colvin. The other three are happily thriving here but I want to leave faster than I got here.

"Aaron, is the baby here yet? Did we miss it?" I hear Mom saying breathlessly from behind me. I turn towards the front doors and see the rest of my family running in the doors like a pack of dogs being let out of the pen. I smile at the thought and just shake my head no.

"The nurse said she'd come and update us as often as she can. Aud wouldn't let me go in either."

"I'm so very glad you're here Aaron. You'll get to see your first nephew hopefully before you leave." Mom says with a big smile and hugs me before sitting down in the chair next to mine.

"I'm glad I was here to help get them to the clinic. Not sure Maysen could have done it without passing out. He looked a little green."

"He just loves your sister so much. After what they went through to get back to each other, it's just so sweet how protective he is of her."

"I'm glad to know she found a good guy. I'm going to go for a walk and make some calls."

I walk back out the front doors and pull my cell phone out of my pocket. I dial my secretary's number and wait for her to answer.

"Hello Aaron. How was the trip to Oklahoma?"

"Hi Monica. It was good thanks."

"And the wedding? Was it beautiful?"

"It was great. Got here just as they started."

"That's great. What are you doing calling me? Shouldn't you be celebrating with your family?"

"I'm actually in the hospital with my sister and her husband. I drove them here tonight to have the baby. She's in there now."

"Never a dull moment with you is there?"

"Seems to be that way. What I'm calling for is I was hoping you could exchange my flight for something leaving soon. I need to get back to work."

"Aaron, things are handled here. You don't have to rush back. Take your time and enjoy your family. Your flight doesn't leave for another two days."

"I need to fly back ASAP. I have a lot of paperwork left to take care of. I'll wait to hear from you about the new flight. Thanks Monica."

"Are you sure Aaron? I know for a fact you haven't been home for a long time. Don't you want to see your sister's child?"

"No, I need to get back to work. Like I said, I will wait to hear from you. Email the itinerary to me and I'll see you as soon as I get back."

"Whatever you say Aaron. I'll let you know. Give me a few minutes, its ten o'clock at night here."

"Very good thank you. Sorry it's so late."

"Goodbye Aaron."

I hang up the phone and expect to feel guilty for calling Monica so late but I don't. All I feel is the urge to get out of this place and fast. I feel like this town is sucking the life out of me. I can't breathe and I don't like it at all. This is exactly the reason I left for college and never moved back. I can't imagine being here full time. No way. My family might love it but I do not. Quicker I can get out of here the better. Now to break the news to my family that I'm leaving soon. Tonight wouldn't be soon enough.

***

"Where did everyone go? The food that bad?" I hear from behind me coming from the back door to the barn.

"No silly, they all went to the hospital or clinic or wherever people have babies around here. Amelia's daughter went into labor." I tell one of the workers.

"Are they coming back or is the party over?"

"We can get the place cleaned up so that when they do end up getting back they won't have to worry about a thing."

The worker which I think his name is Miguel walked back into the makeshift kitchen area to get the staff informed of the new plans. We should be out of here in a couple of hours tops. I hope we can get it all taken care of before Amelia comes back. One less thing for her to worry about would most likely be best. She must be sick with worry and so excited all in one.

Thinking about the worried mother hanging around the hospital awaiting her grandchild makes me sad. I know that my own mother will never be present for anything like that. Heck I'm not sure I'll ever have children at all. Not sure that's in the cards for me. After my parents were killed in a plane crash when I was 3 years old, I went from foster home to foster home until I was 18 and went to college. Not sure I'll ever want to bring another child into a world like this one's becoming. Living without parents is one of the toughest things I've had to face so far in my 29 years. Not having that parent there to tell about your new job or to ask questions about a recipe that you love. I can't imagine bringing a life into this world without a guarantee that I'll be around forever. I know, that sounds stupid but I really can't have a child that will be left to live the life I have. That would be selfish of me to do. I won't do that. Children are beautiful and wonderful but I'll just enjoy everyone else's kids and be happy with that. I am okay with that.

"Amie? Earth to Amie." I snap out of my pity party and see that Miguel is back again looking at me like I have two heads.

"Sorry, I was thinking about what needs to be done." He looks at me with a skeptical look on his face. Yep, he didn't buy my excuse and I feel my face redden with embarrassment.

"Yeah ok. Well, the crew is ready to take the tables down and load the chairs. Is that okay?"

"Yes, that's perfect I'll help them with that. Thank you Miguel." He walks off shaking his head clearly thinking I'm losing my mind. I probably am.

***

Sitting in the chair next to Mom fifteen minutes later I get a text from Monica.

> *Only flight left leaves Tulsa at 6 am. Sorry. Email flight info in a few.*

Awesome. That's not soon enough but it'll work. It's almost 10 o'clock here so I really should go back to the ranch and get my stuff. I can leave from the clinic in the morning. Who knows how long Audrey's going to take to have this kid.

I could just leave for the airport now and sleep there. Why didn't I think of that before?

"Mom, I have to go but tell Audrey congrats and that I love her. Send me lots of pictures." I try to hug her but she's looking up at me with the most pitiful look on her face.

"You're leaving now? I thought for sure you'd be here for a few days Aaron! Audrey's having your first nephew in there and you're leaving?" Ok so I feel a little guilt this time. But I still need to go.

"I'm sorry Ma but I've got to get back. I've got tons of paperwork piled up for this new contract we landed. I would stay if I could Ma but I can't. I love you though." She stands up and I give her a hug knowing I'm a terrible son who just lied to his mother. It would break her heart to know I don't want to be here. Especially since I changed my three day trip to a one day. What she doesn't know won't hurt her. Right?

"Oh Aaron. I really wish you would stay and at least see the baby. Your sister would really like you to be here too. We all would." She starts to tear up and I really feel the urge to get out of here.

"Sorry Ma. I'll call Aud when I can. Love you all so much. Take care." I back towards the door and see everyone waving goodbye looking like I was leaving for war. I'm only going a plane ride away, goodness.

Hopping into my rental car I feel a sense of excitement to be getting away. The city limits of Colvin in my rear view mirror has always been what I've longed to see. The world is so much bigger than this small town and I've felt so free being away from the confines of it.

I push the gas pedal down a little harder than needed but it makes my heart pump faster.

2

I write each paycheck and my heart hurts because I'll barely have enough left over to get food and gas for the week. I need to find somewhere local and get my business set up. Need to, but how?

I've been working out of my car for the past six months so I'm not able to have tables or even napkins on hand like I would if I had an actual space for my business to be. I just pray no one realizes that I'm living in my car because who'd want to hire a bum?

As I see them pull away I get a twinge of jealousy in my gut as they head onto their warm and cozy homes. I'm heading to my cramped car and maybe the park tonight. I should be able to park there again without anyone realizing I'm there. This will be four times this week that I've parked there and used the restrooms to bathe and change each morning. It would be so embarrassing if someone found my secret out. Too embarrassing.

I walk to my car and pause for a minute to look around the 6AB Ranch. This is such a large place and feels like such a wonderful place to live. They don't realize how good they have it with such a wonderful place to call home. I could only dream of living somewhere like this. At this point in my life I would go for any type of a home other than my little beat up car. Sleeping in total fear of someone finding me out is exhausting. Can life get any worse?

My parents were killed in a car wreck when I was very young leaving me to live in the foster system. I moved from foster home to foster home never knowing where I was going to end up. Once I reached 18 I was free to do whatever it was I wanted to do. I was very lucky to find out that I could apply to college and get grants and scholarships to do so. Without them I wouldn't have been able to go to college or even have the dream of my own business.

When I was in my second year of college at the University of Oklahoma, I was sitting in the library researching a topic for a paper when a young man walked up to my table and asked to share it. He was the most handsome and sweet thing I had ever met. He introduced himself as Brady Carlyle from Wichita, KS. He was also studying to get his business degree at OU and we seemed to have a lot of the same classes together. We hit things off quickly and started dating a few weeks later. We were together throughout all of college and when we both graduated on the same day, Brady proposed that we move into a house together. He was from a wealthy family that had already bought him his first town house there in Norman.

After about a year and a half together, his family was in town one weekend for a charity golf tournament so Brady thought it was time for all of us to meet. Needless to say, his parents were not very happy with my orphan status. From the start, they didn't feel that I was the right fit for their son and never supported our relationship. That never stopped us from loving each other, but it was always at the back of our minds. The next Christmas, Brady proposed to me and his parents went nuts. They threatened to disown him and take away his trust funds if he married me but that once again didn't stop Brady. We were slowly planning our wedding and working on starting a party planning business together. Brady wanted to get my business up and running before we got married so that I would always have something to fall back on.

That was put to a sudden halt one April morning. It was a Saturday which was also my birthday and Brady left early that morning before I woke up and went to the nearest outdoor flower vendor to get me some flowers. He was standing and paying for them when a man walked up behind him and drew a gun. He robbed Brady and the man who owned the flower market. When Brady put up a fight, the man shot him and ran; never looking back.

I got that dreaded phone call from the police department that no one ever wants to get. "I'm sorry ma'am but your fiancé was killed today. We need you to come down to the morgue and identify his body. We are very sorry for your loss." Just thinking about it gives me the chills and my hands start to shake.

I called Brady's parents and of course they blamed it all on me since he was out getting flowers for me. They cleaned out our town house and kicked me out without a penny to my name. All of the plans that Brady and I had were torn to shreds and our life together was as if it never happened. I was left penniless and heartbroken. They wouldn't even allow me to attend his funeral. That was just as painful as being left orphaned when my parents died. All I could do was find odd jobs and sleep on my friend's couch until I figured things out.

It took me a few months before I was able to get my own little apartment but things weren't always easy. I finally found the party planning assistant position in Tulsa so I moved there a few years ago. I was starting to get a little more comfortable with my life when the company downsized and most of us were laid off. I of course was one of them and couldn't afford my apartment anymore. Therefore I had to move everything into my car to live which I still am. I've been roaming around Oklahoma trying to find my place when I stumbled upon Colvin and then upon Amelia Blake. My saving Grace.

***

Home Sweet Home. Right. I walk in the front doors of my penthouse apartment and immediately remember the reason I left for Colvin to begin with. The apartment is nothing but an empty shell; walls, ceiling and a floor. Absolutely nothing else. I walk into my bedroom and see the mattress on the floor with an alarm clock plugged into the wall and a few suits and ties in the closet. Necessity. Nothing more, nothing less. My family would be so shocked to see that I don't live the lavish lifestyle I used to. Heck I'm shocked every time I walk out of those elevators doors. What happened to me? Why am I at the bottom again? I haven't been this way since I graduated from college. How did I get this way?

Poker. My love of the game has gotten me here. I never turn down a chance to play. Even when the stakes got higher and higher. I win my fair share but I lose even bigger. Once my secret whirlwind wedding and divorce happened, I turned to the dark side. I turned dark myself.

I met Miss Payton Delaney in Miami when her father hired AB Construction to revamp his office building. She was a gorgeous blonde that knew just what she wanted. Me. I couldn't fight her off and eventually gave in and once I did there was no stopping that freight train. We married in one of those tacky little Vegas chapels and divorced just as quickly. Divorced once she realized I wasn't her 'happily ever after'. She tried taking every penny I owned and I really didn't fight her either except for when it came to AB Construction. She knew she would never get that so she took all the bank accounts and houses. I kept the company and the penthouse apartment. She never wanted children either and when she did get pregnant, she took care of it, as she said. I was devastated but she was relieved.

That was three years ago. A lot has changed in those three years. She would turn her nose up at me if she saw this place now or who I have become. I guess I should be relieved there isn't a child that has to see me in this state, but it still makes my heart ache when I think of what having that child would have been like.

I feel my phone buzz which rips me out of my mental horror movie. I look at it and see it's a text from an old friend in Vegas.

> *Poker tournament. BIG $$. Tonight. Same place same time. U in?*

I read the words a few more times. If I could just win one of those big money pots I could get things back on the straight and narrow. Things would then get back to normal. I can win, I just know I can.

> *Yes. I'm in. What's the buy-in?*

> *20 k. Got u down. c u tonight.*

Twenty thousand dollars? Holy crap. That's about all I have left in my checking account. Just enough for a plane ticket and the buy in. Let's do this. We're gonna win it all back. We are. We have to.

***

I recline my passenger seat as far as it'll go and try to relax. No one will find me here tonight. I need to get some rest but my eyes just won't close. I turn my head towards the window in time to see a star shoot across the dark night sky. The child in me wants to make a wish but the down-on-your-luck adult thinks there's no use. I'm not foolish enough anymore to think wishing upon a star will make my dreams come true. Dreams only get shattered by angry adults. I breathe in deep and exhale slowly. I used to have such big dreams but now I pray no one finds out that this small four door car is my home and transportation.

***

After leaving the clinic late that night Amelia drives by the south side of the park and sees a familiar little car. Amie. What's she doing parked here so late? Surely her car didn't break down. Amelia drives in the park entrance and over towards Amie's car. Once she parks next to it she gets out praying that no one vandalized it while it's been sitting here.

But as she gets up to the driver's side window, she sees a small body lying in the other seat. Amie's asleep in her car? Amelia looks in the backseat and sees clothes and shoes along with towels and necessities needed for a normal day. What in the world is going on? Why is she sleeping in a parked car? Is she living in her car?

Amelia puts her hand to her mouth to cover the gasp when she finally realizes that Amie really is living in this small car. "Oh that poor girl." Amelia says to herself and climbs back into her own car, heart breaking as the full weight of the situation hits her. But instead of feeling sorry for Amie she immediately moves into savior mode and brainstorms all the way to the ranch about how to change Amie's living arrangement.

3

After six rounds my piles of chips are taller than the rest of the players at the table. If I cashed them in now I'd have won my buy-in back plus about three times. That would pad my account quite nicely; I should cash out. But if I win a few more rounds it would get even better. I've been on a roll so what would a few more hurt?

"Deal me in." I say and accept my cards. A few players say they're out leaving only myself and two others. One man I've seen before at the table but the other I haven't.

"How're you gentlemen tonight? My name's Roger Harrington." The familiar man says as he looks at his cards. He always talks when he has a lousy hand. Always.

"Aaron Blake and I'm good thanks." I look at the unknown man but he's looking at his hand as if no others sit at the table with him. Friendly guy I see.

I win this hand too. Roger went all in and now I've got his chips too. Should be around $120,000 if I were to cash in. I look at Mr. Friendly to decide if I'm cashing out or going another round. Let's go again.

After a few more hands with the two of us left he finally looks up at me with one of those faces that hide any emotion. "All in. You too?"

I've won almost every hand and he's down to very little chips. No brainer. For me.

"You sure about that?" I motion towards his chips.

"Let's go. Life's a gamble isn't it?"

Dealer sends our cards one by one. I pick up mine and see that I've got all low cards. Nothing. Crap. If this last card isn't a good one then I just royally messed up. A 4 of clubs. I have a pair of 2's. Holy crap. If he has anything better than a pair of 2's I am done. Completely done.

"Looks like your luck just changed son." He lays down his hand which includes three kings and rakes up every chip I had. Every. Single. One.

"Tough being the loser isn't it? Not so arrogant and confident are ya?"

I just lost almost $200,000 in one hand. How the heck did that just happen? I've won every other hand since I sat down here. I look up at Mr. Unknown in time to see his evil grin while he works at stacking up all the chips. He played me. He lost all those hands to make me think I was going to win it all. Damn him. No one out plays me. Anger is boiling up inside me and that grin on his face makes me see red.

"Double or nothing." He looks up at me in shock.

"You're a little light on chips my friend."

"I'm not your friend and I'm not losing to a cheater like you."

"Cheater? That's quite the accusation. I'll accept your wager. What do you have that'll be worth my time? The lint on your side of the table isn't worth half a million."

"I have a very successful construction company that's worth three times that."

"That's more than our wager. You have a brain in your head?"

"Life's a gamble. Isn't that what you told me earlier?"

"Deal 'em."

After getting all of my cards and seeing those flipped over by the dealer I feel excitement bubble up inside me. A full house. Mr. Unknown can't have any better than that. I lay my hand down and smile up at him.

"Well, well. That's an impressive hand. Looks like your life just took a dramatic turn where luck is concerned. Royal straight flush. Sorry but you no longer have that construction company. I'll expect your attorney to contact mine by the end of day tomorrow. Nice doing business with you Mr. Blake. Go back to that little small town and lick your wounds."

"How do you know where I'm from? Have we met before?"

"I know you well." I hear a familiar female voice from behind me. Payton. That voice feels as if acid were poured into my ears.

"What the hell are you doing here?" I watch her crack that poisonous smile and walk past me and put her arms around Mr. Unknown. As she presses her lips to his I about lose all willpower to stand. What the heck?

"Watching you get your butt whipped in poker. This is my husband Michael Sands. And he just won me what I was after."

"My company! You set me up!"

"Yes, we knew you couldn't resist. Michael tipped the dealer handsomely to help. I now own AB Construction, thank you."

"You've been after AB since the divorce. You're going to pay for this!"

"And now I have it. Have a happy life Aaron. I know I will."

And they turn to walk away with arms wrapped around each other. How did this just happen?

***

"Amie, hello. What can I do for you?" Amelia says when she answers the phone.

"I just wanted to make sure everything went as you had planned last night. The reception I mean."

"It was wonderful. You and your team did an amazing job thank you. I'm just sorry it was cut short. My new grandson is worth it though."

"I bet he's beautiful. Congratulations." I try to keep my voice from cracking.

"Are you okay honey?"

"I'm fine thank you. Well, if everything was up to your standards then I'll just thank you and be on my way. Thank you for your business and if you are ever in need of an event planner again, please let me know."

"Actually, I have a proposition for you. Do you have somewhere to be?"

"I have some time." A bunch of time but she doesn't need to know that.

"I'm the head of the ladies church group and we need to plan our annual leadership conference for the area members. Would you be interested in helping with that?"

"When is your conference?"

"Two months away. We'd have to work closely together until that day. I don't have time to head that up now with my grandson and all."

"I'll need to check on temporary housing there in Colvin for the time being. I wouldn't want to commute each day for two months."

"You live in Tulsa right?"

"Um, yes ma'am." Please don't ask me where at in Tulsa.

"Where at? I have some relatives that live there." Ugh I knew she would ask.

"Oh just out by the airport. I have to hear those darn planes day and night." I shuffle my feet praying she believes me. I don't know much else about that area, why did I pick it? Dummy.

"I'll make a few calls and let you know what I find. If that's okay with you."

"That would be very helpful thank you."

"Nice talking to you dear. Have a great day."

"You too." Nice day? Oh yes sitting in my car at the Colvin Park is a great time. I pray Amelia can find me somewhere to stay while I'm here helping with the conference. I would give just about anything for a hot shower and a bed to sleep in. Oh wouldn't that be wonderful? A girl can dream right?

4

After a long flight back from Vegas, I lie here on my makeshift
bed and realize that I'm completely broke and all I have is my car.
That's it. I owe the remainder of my lease on this apartment that
was due months ago. I have a few days left before they're going to
kick me out. I have to sell my car. Where the hell else do I get the
money? Where do I go from here? I lost my company, my
apartment, everything. What do I have left?

Home. That's it. I wish that didn't sound as dreadful as it does.
My family will look at me with so much pity and disappointment.

I pull myself up, shower and head out to the Mercedes dealership I
have used so frequently since I made my first sizable paycheck.

"Ah, Mr. Blake. Time to trade up again?" Al has helped me every
time I've come in for years. Every year to be exact. I've traded
my current models for the newest every first business day of
January.

"No, I'm needing to sell this girl. I'm heading out of here on an
extended stay. Can you do that for me?" I lie in hopes he's not
too curious today. How do I explain that I'm flat broke?

"Well, let's go into my office and see what we can do."

"Excellent. Thank you."

A half hour later I walk out of Mansfield Mercedes for what will most likely be the last time. I turn just in time to see them take the car I just parted with into the garage. I'll never feel the soft leather on my skin or grip the sleek steering wheel again; I'm going to throw up. How does one go from complete luxury to the complete opposite? Now I'm left asking for a ride back to the apartment, wow.

I pay off my lease and pack up my belongings into three suitcases. I stand here with bags in hand at the doorway of what used to be home. It feels like someone else's life. It is now. With a big sigh I walk away towards the awaiting taxi. He takes me to the attorney's office to sign the papers I can't believe I'm signing and then to the airport to catch that dreaded flight back to Oklahoma. I just can't believe this is happening.

***

"Amie, its Amelia Blake. I was wondering if you had a few minutes."

"Sure, how can I help you?"

"I would like to propose something to you."

"Another proposal?" I say laughing and her doing the same on the other end.

"Last one, I promise."

"I seem to come out on the good end of your proposals so I'm always up for them."

"This one's about housing. I have an apartment above the garage here at the 6AB Ranch that's now empty since Audrey got married. It's sitting here and I could really use your being close by when we need to meet for the conference details. My schedule is so irregular that it could be any time of day or night when I'll need to see you. What do you say?"

"Wow if you're sure. I'm not sure how much I can pay you for rent, but tell me how much and I'll work it out."

"I don't want you to pay rent. You'd be staying here because of my schedule so it'll be doing me a huge favor."

"You can't be serious."

"I am. You can always help me with other duties in town and around here if you would feel better about it. You can be my personal assistant and party planner. Sound like a deal?"

"That sounds amazing thank you."

"You can move in whenever you're ready. We can get started on the conference as soon as you do. The apartment is ready now so whenever."

"Amelia, I appreciate this opportunity so much. I'll get my apartment packed up and be there by the end of the day. Is that too soon? I don't think I'll need to bring all of my belongings." Liar. I'm such a good liar when I need to be. It's scary. All of my belongings will come with me because they're always with me. In my car.

"Today is fine. Come by the main house when you get here and we'll get your keys and get you settled in."

"Thank you again. Goodbye." This is so amazing and thoughtful. I wonder if she'll notice if I don't bring much more than a box and a suitcase. I pray not.

I can't stop smiling because I'll have a bed and a hot shower tonight. And something other than a public restroom. Using one in the middle of the night is definitely something I won't miss.

"Things are lookin' up kid." I smile and say to myself and start to pack up my items inside the car. Finally a home, even if it is only temporary. I'll take it.

***

"Austin, I'm headed to Tulsa on flight 146. Can you come get me without telling anyone else? I mean NO ONE ELSE!" I yell into my cell phone.

"Man, testy are we? What's got your undies in a bunch? You want a huge favor and you scream at me like that?"

"Sorry. I don't want to talk about it right now. My flight's about to board so I have to go, just promise me you won't say a word."

"Where are you planning on staying after this flight ends with you being in Colvin?"

"I was hoping you would let me crash with you for a few days and let me hide out."

"Hide out? What the heck is going on big brother? Are you running from the law?"

"No you idiot, nothing like that. I'll explain more when my flight gets in. Please."

"Alright, I'll be there but I do have to tell my wife."

"Naturally. But the gag order applies to her too. I know how those women in this family talk."

"See ya in a few hours."

"Thank you Austin."

Later as we circle the Tulsa airport before landing I look out the plane window and see the familiar Oklahoma landscape I've seen hundreds of times before. This time feels so permanent though. It feels like I'm being sent here as a punishment for some big crime. I guess in a way I am. I'm a bit ashamed that I see coming home as a form of punishment but it's true. I dread having to explain the situation to my family. Having to tell Austin and Leah is going to be torture enough. He's waiting at baggage claim with that smug look on his face I'm sure. Grrrr. I am such a loser!

5

"Amie come on in. Always a pleasure to see you."

"Thank you. You're so kind. I'm eager to get busy working on this conference."

"As am I. There will be fourteen churches from the surrounding counties that will be sending their board members to Colvin to attend. Should be a great turn out."

"Sounds exciting. Would you like to get together this afternoon and put some of your ideas on paper?"

"You need to get settled in first. We'll meet tomorrow morning if that works for you."

"Whenever works for you works for me. Please let me know when that is. I owe you so much for finding me somewhere to stay while I'm here in Colvin. I would feel so much better if you allowed me to pay rent."

"Nonsense. You're here to help around my schedule. You're doing me a huge favor."

"If you say so."

"I'll show you the apartment and have a hand bring your stuff upstairs."

"Oh there's no need. I only brought one box, a suitcase and a bag. I can handle it fine. But thank you. You lead the way, I'll follow."

***

As I turn the corner in the airport and enter the baggage claim area, I spot Austin right away. About a foot taller than everyone else and blonde. No wonder he caught the eye of a famous model. My little brother is quite the looker. I chuckle at that thought. I'm not sure why this never occurred to me before but the smile on his face as I get nearer to him surprises me. There is no smug look, just genuine happiness to see me. Me. The world's worst big brother.

We embrace and pat each other on the back. He's even a few inches taller than me. When did that happen?

"Hello big brother. How was the flight? You look like crap." He smiles. Of course he does, the pain.

"Well thanks. Flight was okay but trying to sleep on one of those planes in those tight quarters is just wrong."

"You flew coach? Now you know how we peasants feel." Another grin. I slug him in the shoulder and darn it if I don't smile too. It's infectious.

"I should have three bags. Fetch them would you peasant?" I smile this time before he can. I haven't truly smiled like this for a very long time. It feels foreign but great.

"Let's go Your Highness. I parked the chariot on this end." He grabs one of my bags and me the others. Man have I ever missed this guy. Maybe coming home won't be as bad I originally thought.

"Thanks for the ride Austin. And of course for not ratting me out."

"Of course, but you do realize they'll figure it out. Your secret's safe with us for the time being anyways."

"Thanks. I'm just not ready to go there yet. I need a few days to breathe and figure myself out first."

"I get it. But you're going to have to talk about it at some point. I'm here when you do."

"I know and thanks." That's all I can say and turn to look out the car window. There's that familiar feeling of dread and impending punishment again. I'm terrible. Going home should be happy not this painful. Lord knows my family is Heaven sent. That makes me feel even worse. A lot worse.

***

"This place is wonderful, thank you again Amelia. Anything I can do to help you, please let me know. I owe you so much." I stand inside the front door looking around the most beautiful and spacious apartment I have ever been inside. And never thought I would live in. The bed. The jetted tub. Stainless appliances. Granite counters. Walk in closets. Holy cow I have died and gone to Heaven. Please don't wake me up!

"You are more than welcome honey. I'll let you get unpacked and settled in. Dinner will be at six at the main house. AJ and I would love to have you join us."

"I would love that thank you. I'll see you at six then." I smile as she walks out the front door leaving me alone in my new place. Mine. Wow, unbelievable.

***

"Your room's this way. And before you go in I have to warn you. It's all pink and girly."

"Whoa, you weren't kidding. How do you have such a pretty room in your house man?" I smile and elbow him in the arm.

"It used to be Leah's room when she was growing up. She used to come and spend summers with her grandparents remember."

"Oh yeah. I forgot she was your childhood crush." Another smile. They seem to be coming so much easier now.

"Yes and now I'm married to her and own Stampley's. Can we move on?" He says a little annoyed with me. I chuckle knowing Austin always did get touchy when any of us guys mentioned Leah growing up.

I always wanted him to help me build things but he only wanted to play in the dirt with the weeds and Aidan played with the livestock. I smile again as the memories start running through my head.

"I don't want to know what you're smiling about do I?"

"Just remembering how different the three of us boys were growing up. Each of us wanted such different things out of life."

"And we all achieved them. I own the nursery, Aidan has the AK Ranch and breeding program, and you have AB Construction. We all did well for ourselves don't ya think?" He smiles with pride evident on his face.

Little does he know I'm the biggest screw up possible. Ran home with my tail between my legs just like a whipped pup. Damned Payton! How did I let this happen?

"Are you staying home to babysit me all day?"

"No you idiot. I'm heading to the nursery. Leah's coming home early to get dinner started but I'll be home later. Some of our potting sheds are falling apart. Hey, you should swing by and give me a hand. You're the carpenter extraordinaire."

"We'll see. I'm pooped and wanna take a shower. Maybe tomorrow."

"That works."

"Tell her not to rush home. I'll be fine. Thanks again Austin this means so much."

"Anytime. You're my brother Aaron. I would do anything for you. Just let me know what else you need."

"Will do thanks." I turn and walk the rest of the way into my pretty in pink lodging for the time being. Even the pink ruffles on the curtains are more than I have to my name. Heck I don't even really have that anymore now that my company's gone. I need to take a long hot shower and try to wash away this sappiness that I've got going on. It's pathetic.

6

Knocking on the large double wooden doors of the 6AB Ranch main house, I can't help but wonder how in the world I got here. Last night I was sleeping in my car and starting tonight I will be in my own apartment and my own bed. I can't help but let a big smile slide across my face.

"That smile looks amazing on you Amie. You should smile more often."

Just as I started to smile she opened the door. I must have looked like a fool standing there in la-la land grinning so big. Good grief, way to make a first impression you idiot.

"I'm sorry I was lost in thought."

"No need to apologize. You're a beautiful girl with a beautiful smile. I don't think I've seen you genuinely smile in all the time I've known you. You really should do it more often."

That embarrasses me and I can feel the heat flooding my face and neck. All I can do is look at my feet and mumble, "Thank you."

"No need to be embarrassed. Come on in, dinner's almost ready."

I follow what seems to be the kindest woman on the planet into her dining room. This house is so beautiful I wouldn't begin to know where to explain what I see. To me everything is so homey.

"Your house is amazing Amelia. Is it original to the land?"

"Yes and no. It used to be AJ's great grandfather's ranch but has been passed down through the generations. This has always been the main house but a handful of years ago we had our eldest son Aaron do a complete remodel so that it'll last another couple of generations."

"He did an amazing job. He's the one that has the construction company and works in all the big cities, right?"

"Yes, he's so busy that we don't see him very often. He was actually here for Austin's wedding but left not long after. He did drive his sister and Maysen to the clinic though. We haven't heard from him since. I'm sure he's in a luxurious city doing another big deal."

"Sounds lonely. Is he married or have kids?"

"No, he's the last one of our children that is unmarried. I guess he's too busy to find a wife. I'm not entirely sure he will ever get married."

"That's sad. But some of us just aren't cut out for it."

"Are you married?"

"No. Engaged but never married. Could I help with dinner?" I say desperate to change the subject.

"No, it's all ready. I'll go get AJ, please have a seat. I'll be right back." She smiles but it doesn't make it to her eyes. Pity. I should be used to that look by now. It's still not easy to see or accept.

***

After unpacking and taking a long hot shower, I see I've missed several calls, texts and emails from Monica. Oh boy. I hit redial and held my breath.

"Aaron what did you do? That witch is in here bossing everyone around. She says you gave her the company! Please tell me that's not true and I can kick her butt out of here!" She screams without saying hello first. I should have warned her. I was too caught up in my own misery to think of my loyal employees.

"I'm sorry. It's true. She owns AB now."

"You bet the company and lost, didn't you?"

"Yes. She'll have to pay you a nice severance package if she fires you. Make her life hell and go to the Bahamas. I'm sure working for me night and day has warranted the need for a vacation."

"You I can handle. This she-devil, not so much. Half the workers have already quit. A lot of the vendors refuse to do business with her. She's only been here for two hours Aaron! It's that bad."

"Like I said, I'm sorry. I was reckless and it didn't pay off. You work for her now."

"I'll just come to you and we can start another company. I've been with you from the start of this one. We can do it again."

"No, I don't know what I'm going to do now."

"Where are you? Are you still in the City? I'll come to the penthouse."

"I'm back in Oklahoma for a while. I don't know how long and I really don't know where to go from here."

"You went home? It's that bad? Oh Aaron, did you bet everything?"

"Yes. Sold my car and got a flight here. No one else knows I'm here but Austin. I just need time to come to terms with what just happened."

"Let me know if you need anything. Keep in touch and take care."

"I will. Be careful with the she-devil as you put it." I smile as I envision Payton in a red devil costume with a tail and horns.

Monica can handle Payton. I just hope she doesn't punch her. She's slugged me a few times in the arms and chest when I've made her mad. That makes me smile too. That girl has been there for so much. And I left her alone without even a warning. Smooth move Aaron, even higher loser status now.

***

"Thank you so much for dinner. It was wonderful."

"Amie you're welcome here any time. We have quite the empty nest now so any other company we can have is always a good thing."

"I appreciate the offer. I had better get going. I need to go into town for a few things."

"Well, thanks again for joining us. I'll call you tomorrow with a time for our meeting."

"Very well, thank you." I head out the big doors I came in as quick as I can. They asked so many questions about me and I feel like I was being interrogated by the FBI. I know they were just trying to get to know me, but goodness that made me so uncomfortable. I don't think I'll be going back for dinner any time soon.

I climb into my car and turn the key. Nothing. Wonderful just wonderful. I pound my hand on the steering wheel and let out a frustrated scream. More like a grunt but it was all I could get out. What is next? Oh I am even more thankful for the roof I have over my head now. This would have been even worse if I had been still trying to live in this car.

tap tap tap

I jump out of my skin as I hear the tapping on my window. I turn and see Amelia's husband AJ standing next to me staring. He smiles and motions for me to lower the window. I hit the button but nothing. Duh you idiot, you can't start it because there's no power. I smile feeling stupid, open the door, step out and stare up at the big man I met at dinner.

"I'm sorry to startle you. Amelia said you were headed to town and I saw you sitting here in your car so I thought you might've had trouble."

"I can't get it to start. It won't even make a sound. I'll just wait and call the garage in town tomorrow."

"My son in law owns the garage. I'll have him come get it for you. You can take Amelia's car to town now if you'd like."

"Oh you don't need to do that. I couldn't pay him anyway. I'll wait and hopefully it'll be better tomorrow."

"I believe Amelia's going into town to see the new grandbaby in a few minutes. You could ride with her or she could pick up a few things for you."

"Oh thank you. I'll call her." I step away and walk as fast I can to the apartment. How embarrassing. Here only a couple of hours and already the man is having to handle my business for me. Good grief.

7

"Something smells great Leah. What's that you're making?"

"Thank you. I imagine it's the lasagna you smell. You do like lasagna don't you? I guess I should have asked first."

"I love lasagna. Anything Italian I love."

"Including the women?" She asks with a big mischievous grin.

"Actually I wouldn't know. I went to Italy on business and didn't have time to check out the local beauties."

"Wow, Don Juan didn't go play?" That grin again.

"What is it that my brothers have told you about me? I'm far from a Don Juan. I haven't had the time to be one."

"Ah so you're misrepresented? My apologies sir." And she curtsies. She is perfect for my brother.

"It's obvious now what you two see in each other." I can't help but grin at her too. I could get used to this friendly banter. No wonder all my brothers have dropped like flies, my sisters in law are just as quick with the insults as they are. And my sister, goodness she's got the whole package in a very short amount of time.

"Aaron, you've come out of hiding I see." My brother says from the back door.

"Yes dummy I couldn't stay away from that wonderful smell."

"She cooks a mean lasagna. You'll think you were in Heaven as soon as it hits your taste buds."

"Promise?" I smile back trying to match their playful grins. They both laugh so I must have done it right.

"You just wait. It's going to be a good thing I married her or you'd be wanting to once you taste it!" He says and wraps his arms around his new wife. I try to look away, not wanting to see their sweet moment. But I can't help but look a little too long because that is how marriage is supposed to be. Everything mine wasn't.

***

"Amie, my husband says you may need a ride into town?" Amelia says when I answer my phone a while later.

"No, I think I'm okay. I'll keep going down and trying my car. Surely it will start eventually."

"AJ already had it towed to our son in law's garage in town. I'm sure he'll make sure it's in tip top shape for you. If you really do need to go to town I would be glad to have the company."

"Are you sure you wouldn't mind?" He towed my car? Ugh.

"Not at all. Or I could just pick up a few things for you when I go to the grocery store. Your choice."

"You know, I'm pretty tired. Let me get you some money and a list. I'll bring it right over."

"No hurry. I'll meet you out front of the garage in a few."

She has to be the sweetest woman I have ever met! I wonder if I'll be that type of a mother. What are you thinking about that for Amie? Kids are not in your future. You've decided this.

I make a quick list and grab my last $20 out of my wallet. That's all that's left and I don't know how I'm going to buy groceries.

"Here's the list and some money. Please let me know if it's not enough."

"Milk, cereal, eggs, bread, peanut butter and jam. That's it?"

"Yes ma'am. That's all I need for right now. Thank you." I turn away before the burning can show on my face from the embarrassment that those are the only things I can afford to buy.

"Ok, I'll be back later. Take you a nice long bubble bath. I think you'll enjoy it."

"Thank you again. I think I'll do just that." This time I walk away without turning back around.

***

"So, I'm supposed to go to Audrey's and see the baby. Your mom's headed into town to do just that. Do you want to go meet your nephew Aaron?"

"Leah, he'll go when he's ready. No pushing." He kisses her on the head and ushers her out the front door. I can't imagine going

43

over there right now. Mom would be all over me about what I'm doing home and how long I'm staying. I don't have the heart to tell her I honestly don't know what I'm going to do now.

Once they pull away I stand in their living room looking around at the comfortable home that Austin and Leah have started. It's so much different than my penthouse apartment was. It feels like there's love in every inch here. I walk to the fireplace and run my hand over the picture they have there from the wedding. They're looking at each other so much in love you can clearly see it. My insides start to ache for something like that but I should know by now I'm not that type of guy. I only know how to attract the rotten ones.

I decide to watch a little TV to distract me from my own misery. The first thing I see is the Tulsa news channel and of course there's nothing but bad news to report. I turn it and find the do-it-yourself channels that always seem to calm me. This one has a family that was hit by a tornado last year that's getting surprised with a new house. That really hits me and I wonder if that's something I should have done instead of chasing the money. I might be a more fulfilled man if I had. Money might be nice but it's not rewarding like helping someone else who desperately needs it.

Sighing, it comes to me that I need to get back into what got me started in the beginning. Building things with my own bare hands instead of ordering around a crew and flying all over to attend meetings in high rise offices. That's the part that got old. Only in each place long enough to walk in and out of the meetings. I might have been all over the U.S. and the some of the world but I never enjoyed seeing it.

Austin said he needed help with some of the sheds at the nursery. That would be a great way to start. I'll have to get a tour tomorrow. I actually feel a little bit of excitement brewing over this hard labor that needs done. It feels a bit more comfortable too. It's another feeling I think I could get used to.

I watch a few more episodes and before I know it I feel the most relaxed I have in years. When Austin and Leah come in the front door I realize I've been sitting here the whole time. While they come in like a whirlwind kissing and touching, they barely see me and both turn bright red but continue on upstairs to the master bedroom. I just smile and shake my head. I think I'll stay down here for a while and not in the vicinity of their room. Chuckling, I relax back into the couch and get engrossed into another few episodes.

***

"Amelia? What's all this? I know the money I gave you wouldn't buy all of this. You didn't need to bring me so much." I say in complete shock at the amount of grocery bags she and AJ bring inside the apartment. I try to keep them from entering because this can't be real. I have never had this many groceries.

"Oh nothing for you to worry about sweet girl. I was going to stock the fridge before you got here anyway, so I took the opportunity to do it now. You're not upset are you?" She puts her three bags down on the island counter in the kitchen and takes my hands in hers.

"Upset? Of course not. It's the nicest thing anyone has ever done for me. But I'm a little unsure of what I did to deserve such a wonderful person in my life. Thank you so much." I give her the biggest hug I can muster. This woman was definitely Heaven sent.

"Well, you deserve all of it and more. Never think you're not special. It's just groceries anyway, not diamonds." She smiles at me and starts to put the goods away.

I just stand here watching because to be honest, I don't have a clue where this kind of stuff goes. Peanut butter, jelly and bread are the most I've known and now there's everything a store can offer being put into my pantry. I shake my head because this has to be a dream, what have I done to deserve this wonderful place?

"All set honey. I'll see you in the morning and we'll have that meeting. Sleep well." She kisses my cheek and walks out the front door. I stay in the same position feeling like I'm in a whirlwind dream. I feel my face turning up at the corner with a smile. A rare smile because this really is a big dream come true for me. The apartment itself is amazing but now the grocery store was delivered to me too. Unbelievable. I will definitely sleep well tonight.

***

"You're up early big brother." Austin says as he comes into the kitchen the next morning where I'm having a cup of coffee.

"Used to being up early. My body doesn't know I'm on vacation."

"Vacation? Is that what this little visit is?" He lifts an eyebrow at me wondering if I'm going to talk.

"Nice try. I was thinking I would come help you work on those repair projects you have at the nursery."

"Really? I'd appreciate that. We'd like them to last a little longer than a couple of days."

"You never were the most patient with a hammer."

"Still not. I'm heading over now if you want to ride with me."

"Let's go." I follow him out the front door to his pickup. I see the 'Stampley's Nursery' logo on the side and can't help but smile. He really has accomplished what he wanted to even as a child.

***

I awake in a panic the next morning afraid someone's going to find me asleep in my car. I sit up in bed and look around the room unsure of where I am. This isn't my car. Then it hits me. The

46

events from yesterday replay in my head and I relax knowing I'm safe in my new apartment. My apartment. That makes me smile and I lie back down and snuggle into the covers. This is Heaven.

I slip in and out of sleep for a while before my phone rings. I roll over and reach for it.

"Hello?"

"Amie, I didn't wake you did I?" Amelia of course.

"No, what can I do for you?"

"I was hoping you could come with me today to the church and meet everyone. We can also look over the space where we normally hold the conference."

"Of course. I can be ready in about an hour."

"See you out front in an hour honey." Such a lovely woman.

I smile and get myself up and head to the amazing shower this master bathroom has in it. It's bigger than my car I think.

Stripping out of my clothes and stepping into the warm water makes me finally relax the tension that I've been holding onto for so long. The world has finally turned around for me and I couldn't be more appreciative. I stand under the spray and pray to God that I'll be able to stay here awhile. I'll do everything I can to make it worth Amelia's time to have me here. And rent free? Crazy.

8

After spending a couple of days following Amelia around and making plans for the conference, I'm completely exhausted. That woman is a whirlwind. Luckily today she is babysitting her grandchildren so she'll be busy and I can have a day to recover. I smile when I think of what's gone on the past couple of days.

I walk into the kitchen and decide there's nothing I really want to eat in here so I'll just go to town and eat at Sally's. Thankfully AJ brought my car back yesterday and I won't have to hitch a ride. Grabbing my keys off the hook by the door I smile and head to my car.

Sitting in the driver's seat brings back memories of the way life was before the 6AB. I used to live out of this car and sleep in it too. After having the comforts of the new apartment I honestly can't believe I did live in here for so long.

I shake my head to clear those unpleasant thoughts and start the car. I shift into drive and head to town determined to have a good day but can't help but tell myself, "You better not get used to this life, once the conference is over they'll kick you out." I frown and hope I can save up enough from this job to maybe get my own apartment when that happens. Hopefully.

Before I know it I've pulled up in front of Sally's and it feels like my mouth started to water as soon as I did. Amelia brought me in here yesterday for lunch and I fell in love with the food and the people inside. Everything about this town makes you feel at home. If only I could stay, that would be great.

***

"Looking good brother." I hear Austin say from behind me where I'm finishing up the last potting shed. I've done repairs on the ones that needed it the past couple of days. It's been great getting my hands dirty again.

"Thanks. This one's about done. What else did you need done?"

"Ummm, well we haven't discussed anything else but I'm sure there's a lot more. With this old building I'm sure you could find things to keep yourself busy for months. Especially stuff we've never even thought of."

"I'll take a look around when I'm done here."

"We really appreciate all your help Aaron."

"It's the least I can do since you're housing and feeding me. You're also hiding me from the world."

"True. You do realize they're going to find you out. Each one stops by here all times of the day without warning."

"I'll take my chances."

"Don't say I didn't warn you." That was an evil grin. He's up to something. Who knows what.

I go back to fixing the loose door hinge and feel content doing the manual labor myself. I could really enjoy this again. Hmmm.

***

After enjoying my meal at Sally's I decide I'd like to get Amelia some flowers or a plant as a "Thank You" gift for all she's done for me. She mentioned that her daughter in law and son owned the local nursery so that's where I'll go find what I need. Maybe they can help me pick out something she'll like.

Walking into the nursery I can't help but be in awe of how many rows of gorgeous flowers and greenery there are. And it smells like Heaven in here. If you could bottle that scent and make a perfume someone would be rich. Or maybe they already have, I wouldn't know. Perfume's a luxury I haven't had in a long while.

"Can I help you find anything in particular?" A tall man says as he walks towards me. I vaguely remember him from his wedding reception I did not too long ago. Austin if my memory serves me right.

"No thank you. I would actually like to roam around if that's okay with you."

"Perfect. Let me or my wife know if you do need any help."

"Thank you." Wow he's one handsome flower man. I remember back to that night and see another handsome Blake's face. Goodness that man was scrumptious too. There's something in the water at the 6AB Ranch to create such beautiful human beings.

I walk around for a while and eventually get to the last aisle where I see I'm blocked in by a man high on a ladder. Turning to go back the way I came from, I hear a familiar voice and can't help but look up praying it is him. Aaron Blake the too busy to come home son is here in Colvin's nursery on a ladder handsome as ever. Whoa be still my heart.

"Well hello there. Planning another party?" He smiles wide and my insides twist into a knot. Those eyes and that smile kill me. I feel myself blush as he steps down the ladder and stands in front of me.

"No. Yes. Well, I'm working on a conference with your mother but I'm here today to get her something as a "Thank You" for being so wonderful to me."

"She loves every kind of flower. Tell Austin to make you a 'Mama's Special'. He'll know what you want."

"Ok, thank you. What are you doing here? I hadn't heard from Amelia that you were back in town."

"She doesn't know. No one but Austin does. Ssshhh don't rat me out." He puts his finger against his lips as he says that and I feel my heart start to race again and my mind goes fuzzy.

I look up at him and he's staring at me like I should be saying something. Oh maybe because I should. I'm standing here staring like some dumb teenager.

"Umm, why wouldn't you want your family to know you're here? They love you. You know what? I'm sorry that's none of my business."

"It's alright. You're right though, I just need a little time to figure things out before I see my family."

"Your secret's safe with me. Good luck figuring your stuff out. You have an amazing family. Take care and thanks for the help with the flowers."

"See you around. Amie right?"

"Yes. Surprised you remember that."

"I always remember a beautiful girl's name." And he winks. Oh my goodness.

"I'm sure you do!" I laugh and walk back up front fully aware that he is watching my every move. Why didn't I wear something hot today? Instead just these dumb old khakis?

"Hey now. Insult and walk away?" I look back to see him smiling a cocky and ornery smile. Oh my goodness I could melt.

***

"So, you're helping customers now? Or just the pretty one that came in today?" Austin says on the drive to his house that night.

"She was getting something for our mother you moron so I offered her advice on what to get."

"Mama's Special? Only we kids know what that is."

"Hence the reason I told her to tell you what I did."

"Uh huh. She blushed when she told me who told her about it. Did you hit on her?"

"No dummy. I simply helped out a customer that needed assistance." I can't keep the smile off of my face this time.

"Right." Austin walks away shaking his head once we get to his house. I continue to smile knowing I shamelessly flirted and my little brother knows me so well. Even after all this time. I sure did miss him.

***

"Oh Amie these are beautiful flowers! Austin must have helped you. He knows just what his Mama likes!"

"Yes. Your children know their mother." I wanted so badly to tell her that it was Aaron that got credit here but I promised not to spill his secret.

"Thank you so much. They sure brightened my day." She gives me a big hug and my heart feels a little jolt from all the love that this woman possesses. It makes me wonder if my own mother's hugs would have been this powerful. Of course they would have. She loved me just as fiercely as Amelia loves her family. It might have been a long time since I've felt one of those powerful hugs but her love is something I can't forget.

"You are very welcome. Just wanted to show you how much I appreciate all of your kindness and all you've done for me."

"Anything you need I'm always willing to help."

"Well, I need to work on the conference plans a bit before dinner. Glad you like the flowers." I walk out the door and towards my own home. It's crazy how quickly I became used to having it.

Once I reach the front door I open it and walk into the kitchen and look out the window. From this window I can see for miles and miles where the Blake's own every one of them. It looks so peaceful out there and I can't help but sigh with contentment. It's been so long since I've felt content. I would never have guessed I'd like living so far from anything. I actually love being able to sit out on the balcony and hear nothing but cows, horses, frogs and birds. Yes, the coyote howls late at night were something to get used to but now I don't even notice. I could see myself living here forever. Forever? Don't get too comfortable Amie. This isn't your family and you can't stay here. Especially not forever.

9

"You've done a great job at the nursery Aaron. Thank you so much for the help. Your brother couldn't have accomplished half of what you have." Leah says with a smile as she sets the last of our breakfast on the table. Austin and I are already seated and I see him stick his tongue out at her and smile.

"It was fun. I'll be done today. Have you two thought about a total remodel? That building is shot and a lot of things are going to start getting worse."

"We have, yes. I was always hoping my big brother would do the remodel but he has always been away and busy."

"Was. I'm here now. We can start talking plans and what you envision. I'll think about it too."

"That would be awesome Aaron! I think Audrey and Maysen were talking about building a new place for the repair shop too. We could keep you busy for years with just the family projects. Not to mention the stuff the church and community would want. But, you would have to come out of hiding for that."

"I know. I was thinking of going to the ranch this afternoon after I finish up at the nursery."

"Really? Mom will be so happy to see you home."

"I know." I decide that's enough of that conversation. I shove a mouth full of pancakes in and pray they get the hint.

***

"So, I was thinking we could have the teal table covers, white linens, white assorted flower centerpieces and silver place settings for the brunch. We could have silver chair covers with teal ribbons if you wanted to go that fancy." I finish my presentation with the design board that has all the necessary vision pieces on it.

"Oh Amie! That all sounds exactly like what we had envisioned. You have done an amazing job. We can start ordering whenever you're ready. We'll let you go do your thing now."

"I think that's a good next step. I can inspect the pieces as they come in and re-order if anything needs to be. I've found that sometimes things just aren't what they seem like in the catalogs."

"It's your baby from here on out. We can't wait to see how it all comes together on the day of the conference."

"Thank you. Let me know if you have any changes. I'll get back to work on all of this as soon as I get back home."

"We are all very impressed with the work you have done. You have such an eye for this."

"I love what I do. I'll keep you posted. Thanks again ladies for the opportunity." I pack up my stuff and head to my car full of excitement for this project. I love my job. I love my life.

***

"Well, well who do we have here?" I hear my father's voice coming from behind me in the nursery office.

"Hey Dad. How are you?" I wipe off my hands before I give my old man a hug.

"I'm doing just fine but I have to ask what you're doing here."

"I know. I planned on going to the ranch later today. Do you have a minute?"

"For you son, I always have a minute." He pats me on the back and we walk towards the storage area.

"Dad, I really screwed things up. Royally."

"What do you mean? Did you just get in today?"

"No. I've been here about a week. I'm staying at Austin's. Don't get mad at him, I begged him to keep quiet until I was ready to tell everyone what I'm doing home."

"What's up Aaron? It must be bad to bring you back here. We were thinking we'd never see much of you ever again."

"I know. I've been a horrible son and brother. I just got so wrapped up in my business and life away from here that I forgot what I left behind. I lost everything Dad. I'm flat broke."

"Everything? How did that happen? You owned the company."

"Did own it yes. I had a slight, well serious I guess, poker addiction. I stupidly bet my company and lost."

"Oh my son. That's not good. Are you sure you can't get it back? Didn't you just land a new contract? Have money in savings or retirement?"

"I did yes. But I've wagered it all over the last year. Dad I blew it. No one else to blame but me."

"Wow Aaron. I really don't know what to say except I'm sorry. I'm glad you came home though. Just wish you would have come to the ranch instead of hiding out. But I have to say I understand it was an adjustment for you and weren't ready to talk about it yet."

"I haven't even told Austin. I'm so ashamed Dad. I'll never sit at another poker table again the rest of my life. The game nearly destroyed me." I look down at my hands which have been twisting around each other.

"Son, you don't have to be ashamed of making mistakes. Life is full of them, sometimes they're little and sometimes they're bigger. You just have to start over. Figure out where you want to go from here."

"Since I've been helping out around here I've kinda enjoyed getting my hands dirty again. I've been thinking that maybe I should start up another construction company but not the same way I had been doing things with AB. Something new and something that helps people instead of stepping on them."

"That sounds like a great plan to me Son. Let me know if I can help in any way."

"Thanks Dad. I'm about done here. Can I get a ride with you back out to the ranch?"

"I'll come back by to get you before I go home. It really is good to see you again Aaron. We've all missed you."

"I have missed you all just as much. I didn't realize it until I was back in Colvin."

Dad walks out the door to his pickup and I can't help but feel so much lighter after telling my Dad all I have been keeping bottled up inside. I will need to tell everyone else now. I let out a deep sigh because I know that's going to be painful.

***

After spending most of my afternoon making orders and finishing my sketches I feel famished. I should have stopped for lunch after the meeting with the ladies at the church but I was too excited to get started. Now I'm paying for it. It will be at least an hour or two before dinner so I'd better get something light. I walk to the kitchen and as I'm filling up my glass with water I see AJ's pickup pull up in front of the barn. And out of the passenger side I see the most beautiful man I've ever seen. Again.

He's even smiling. He must have come clean. I don't see Amelia around so I'm going to guess she doesn't know yet that her eldest child is home.

He leans into the back of the pickup and hoists a bale of hay out of it and it's as if it weighs nothing. He is such a strong and sexy hunk of flesh. Oh my goodness. I can see the muscles bunch up on his arms as he throws it down on the others. He wipes his hands on that butt. Oh my what I wouldn't do to put my hands on his butt!

Oh. My. Goodness. Amie. What are you doing? What are you thinking? This man is your employer's son and not just a hunk of meat. You should be ashamed of yourself. It's been way too long since you've been with a man and you know they'll only hurt you. A man in your future doesn't exist. Quit gawking at this one like he's candy.

I shake my head and peek one last look before going back to my desk in the study. I take a deep breath and try to calm the pulses going through me. Get a grip on yourself or you're going to ruin everything you've got going on here.

***

"Can you help me get these bales stacked over there? I'm not as nimble as I used to be."

"Of course Dad. Any help you need just let me know. I have a lot of make-up work to do. Been a long time since I've helped around the ranch."

"You've been busy living your own life Son. We don't blame you for that. It's what we raised you to do."

"Yes, but I blew it big time. Made a colossal mistake and I'm paying for it now."

"It's good to have you home though while you figure it out. You about ready to see your Mama?"

"Yes sir. You go ahead and call her and have her come down here."

"Hey honey, I've got a surprise for you down here at the barn. Yes, now please. Ok see you in a few."

I hear my Dad say into his cell phone when he calls Mom. I think after all these years he still loves to spoil and surprise her. A pang of longing hits way down inside my cold heart but I shove it farther down. This kind of a relationship isn't for you Aaron. You had your chance and blew it.

"She'll be here in a few minutes. She was just putting dinner in the oven. She's going to be over the moon to see you here Aaron."

"I know. I can't wait to wrap these arms around her and see that electric smile so big it could light up the night."

"She does have one of those amazing smiles doesn't she? It's what caught my eye all those years ago. I saw her smiling across the corral and had to talk to her. Sure glad I did."

"Awe Dad that's sweet. Let's stop there though. I really can't handle the gushy stuff right now."

"Why's that son? You haven't had a girl in your life since college. Have you?"

"Let's not talk about that now. Mom's coming I can hear her singing." I smile at the memory of Mom watering her flowers and singing away when we'd get off the bus.

"AJ? Where are you honey?"

"In the tack room." He smiles at me and points toward the door where Mom's about to come through. I turn around and get ready for the excited look on her face.

"In here? I don't...." And she stops speaking and looks at me as if she doesn't recognize me.

"Ma? You okay?"

"Oh my goodness Aaron James Blake what are you doing here? I didn't know you were coming home for a visit!" She flings her arms around me and I can't help but smile. This woman is the only one I can ever count on. This woman only.

"Hey Ma. Are you surprised?"

"Very! AJ you ornery old coot. Why didn't you tell me my oldest son was coming for a visit? I would have whipped up his favorite dessert for tonight."

"No need to go to any trouble Ma. I'm here for longer than a little visit. We'll go through all that later. I'll let Dad fill you in and then I'll tell the kids when they get here."

"Kids? Oh you mean your siblings? I'll call and have them all come tonight for dinner."

"I figured you would. Dad, I'll let you tell her while I run up and shower." This is NOT going to be fun.

10

After finally getting all the orders placed and everything organized for the conference I stand up and feel like I've been hunched over a computer all day. I think a hot bubble bath is exactly what I need. Baths have become my favorite indulgence. Only this jetted dream of a tub. I start the water and pour in my new favorite bubble bath while hardly containing my excitement for the little bit of luxury I have coming my way.

I undress and put my clothes in the hamper while taking out the braid my hair has been in today. I see that the tub is almost half full so I decide to get a glass of wine while I wait. I wrap a towel around me and put the robe from the back of the door on and walk to the kitchen. I of course can't help but wonder if Aaron is still out there in the barn doing hot manual labor. Hot manual labor? Is that even a thing? Well he sure would look HOT while doing it. I chuckle a little and start to pour my wine into the glass. Once I have both hands occupied, the towel starts to slip and falls to the floor. I look around but realize it doesn't matter that I have nothing on under this robe. No one will see me. Heck I can walk around naked if I want.

Feeling empowered I strip off the robe and let it fall to the floor too. I feel so free. More free than I have ever felt in my entire life. I like feeling this way. I might have to start walking around naked all day every day. I laugh and shake my head as I walk with my glass of wine to the waiting Heaven in a bathtub completely in the buff.

I step into the hot liquid that I know will make all my sour muscles and cares melt away. As I sink lower and lower into the water I can't help but send up a little thank you. I don't know if Mom and Dad are helping me out here but I sure am thankful.

I've been relaxing in the tub so long that I drank all my wine and feel the water start to get cold. I lift my hands up and see they're all white and wrinkly too. Time to get out. I'm a bit disappointed but know that I can take another one in the morning if I want to.

I stand up out of the water and reach for my towel but it's not there. I know I put a towel there when I started the water. I look all over the room but no towels in sight and notice the robe isn't on the back of the door either. Oh you idiot you dropped them both in the kitchen. Smart. Now how are you going to dry off? I guess it really doesn't matter. I can simply walk to the kitchen and retrieve the towel and robe.

I start to take the first step out of the bathtub when the bathroom door opens. And the hot hunk of man from earlier walks directly in. With nothing but a towel wrapped around his waist!

"What are you doing in here you pervert? Get out!" I yell and drop back into the water. Well, it would be barely any water since I pulled the plug on it before I got out. Ok so I drop back into a mostly empty bathtub to get out of sight. How can this be happening?

***

I walk out of the barn and grab my bags from the back of Dad's pickup. I could stay in my old room but I think I'd rather be alone than have Mom smothering me all day.

I'll shower and change in the apartment above the garage. Audrey moved out with Maysen after they got married so there won't be anyone there to bother me. I love my family but I've been alone too long to have them under foot.

I wonder if Mom has it unlocked? I walk up to the door and see it's locked. The extra key always used to be under the flower pot on the stairs so I lift it up and there it is.

Inserting the key into the door I look through the glass window and see there aren't any lights on. It's far from being dark but for some reason looking for lights was the first thing I did. Not that anyone would be in here anyway all my siblings have their own houses.

I shut the door behind me and drop the key on the counter. Next I walk with my bags into the nearest bedroom which wasn't the one Audrey used as her own when she lived here. I set my stuff on the bed and start to rummage around for some clean clothes. I'll have to do a load of laundry after the shower so I strip out of the dusty and sweaty clothes I have on. I open the linen closet in the hallway on the way to the master bathroom and wrap a towel around my waist. I know this one has the best shower and the best water pressure.

I don't look around when I walk into the master bedroom but as I reach the door to the bathroom I see it's closed. Why would Mom have it closed? Oh well I'll leave it open when I'm done. She'll never know the difference. I open the door and walk into the room getting the most amazing surprise.

"What are you doing in here you pervert? Get out!" Is all I hear screeching through the room. Standing completely naked and wet is the girl of my dreams. Holy shit she's even more gorgeous when she's naked. And wet oh my goodness!

"Oh my goodness I'm so sorry. I didn't know anyone was in here." I throw my hands up to cover my eyes as she drops into the bathtub. And as I do my own towel drops leaving me also completely naked. Wonderful.

"How did you get in here?" She says and peeks over the side of the tub. Just as my towel leaves me.

"Well isn't that just wonderful. Now we're both naked. I honestly didn't know you were here. What are you doing here?"

"I asked you first!"

"My parents own this place and I needed somewhere to crash and to shower. Your turn."

"I've been staying here while I'm helping your mom. How did you get in? I know I locked that door!"

"The extra key under the flower pot." I look back at her and smile while reaching down for my towel once more. After I get it settled onto my waist again I ask, "Can I get you a towel?"

"I left it in the kitchen with my robe." She says and I can see a blush cover her body.

"Walking around naked were you?" I wink and smile.

"That is none of your business. Would you please go get my towel?"

"I have a better idea. I'll just give you mine." I walk over to the wet goddess and whip off the towel I'm wearing and hand it to her. I see her half lying down in the tub trying to cover all the important parts. She missed getting all of her breasts covered and I have a rough time not staring.

"Could you get out of here? Good grief why are you still in here?"

"Sorry." I walk away towards the kitchen where the other towel is fully aware that she just saw me nude. All of me. But I'm okay with that.

I retrieve the towel and wrap it around my waist like the other one was. I also lift the robe up and head to the bathroom again. This time I knock.

"I have the robe for you if you want it." I stand there and soon the door opens a crack only allowing a feminine hand to escape. She rips the robe out of my hands and slams the door shut again.

"I think I'll use the guest bathroom to shower." And I walk away to do just that. But it's going to have to be a cold one after seeing that gorgeous creature with nothing on but water and suds.

***

I cannot believe that just happened. Oh my goodness. That hunk of a man saw me without my clothes on. And I him. Whoa! This stuff only happens in the movies. I feel like a total moron after flopping myself down in the tub like an embarrassed teenager. I should have stood my ground and made him uncomfortable. He was clearly not uncomfortable.

I groan and put the robe on making sure it's tied as tight as possible. I stand still and listen for the guest shower. Yep, he's in it so I can get dressed in peace. I rush out of the bathroom and rush to shut and lock my bedroom door. Then throw on the shorts and tank top I had planned on wearing faster than I ever have before. Even though the door is locked I can't help but worry he'll come blazing in again and catch me undressed.

I'm buttoning up my shorts when I hear the water turn off from the other bathroom. The hairs on my body stand up as I envision that beautiful male specimen looking into my eyes again with the intensity that seems to always be there. I shiver and shake my head to clear the thoughts. Opening my door I take a deep breath and let it out.

***

Holy crap! I can't believe I just walked in on Amie getting out of the bath. Why didn't I know she was staying here? You haven't been here you jerk how would anyone tell you. It's not like you called home to see what was going on with your family.

This shower really sucks compared to the one in the master bathroom. I had my heart set on all those jets and this has the single shower head above me. Well, should be above me. I have to lean down pretty far to get my hair rinsed. This stupid thing hits me at about the shoulders. I should have just gone into the main house and dealt with everyone. But I would have missed that amazing show I got back there. My mother is going to kill me when she finds out about it. I can't help but smile regardless.

I turn off the water and dry off thinking what a dramatic first meal at home this is going to be. I wrap the towel around my waist and head to the guest room. At least I dropped my stuff in there and not the master. Amie would really have a cow if I invaded that space too. I smile knowing that I enjoy rattling her. She seems so put together and tough as nails on the surface.

As I skip out of the bathroom she's also exiting the master bed-room and looks down at my lack of clothing and grimaces. That is after she checks me out first. I doubt she even realizes she did that.

"Don't you ever wear clothing?" She shrieks and heads to the kitchen. She noticed all right.

"I was just going to get dressed in the guest bedroom. Calm down. You'll be sorry when I cover all this up Missy." I smile and shut my bedroom door. I won. I think.

***

That man never wears clothes. Granted this is the first time I've seen him without them but anyway! Hmph!

I can't stay in this small apartment with a naked man. That is the only thing I am sure of right now. I grab a bottle of water and step out on the balcony. Fresh air that does not smell of clean, sexy man. I feel myself flush again and breathe in deep to get him out of my head.

But I can smell him before I see him walk through the sliding glass doors that lead to the very same balcony I'm on. The one I'm trying to calm down from being around him and his nakedness.

"Look Amie I'm sorry for what happened back there. I honestly didn't know you were staying here. I feel terrible. How can I make it up to you?"

"It's okay I guess. I can't rewind time and not have you see me naked, or me you." I blush even though I really don't want to.

"You're beautiful if that helps any." He smiles that devilish smile and I of course melt again!

"Thanks but it doesn't. Your mom told me no one would be here either."

"Please don't tell my mother. She'll kill me if she finds out I did that and embarrassed her favorite guest."

"I'm not telling her that, it's embarrassing!" An even darker shade of red.

"Whew and I thought for sure you would march right on over there so she would come whoop me!"

"Haha no. I'll get over it, eventually. If you weren't looking at me like you want to rip the clothes off that I have on now, it would help."

"I can't help it. That was the greatest moment of my life!"

"Oh please! You're such a player!" I get up and head back inside but soon Aaron steps in front of me before I can get inside the house.

"I am far from a player. After dinner I'll open a bottle of wine and we can get to know each other. Since we're going to be roomies."

"Excuse me? Roomies? How do you figure?"

"I need somewhere to stay while I'm figuring things out and you have a spare room. Sounds like a win-win to me. Don't you agree?"

"Um. Um. Um. I have to go." And I walk out the door and into his parent's house where I seem to be a part of the big homecoming for the world's biggest pain in the butt. My butt right now. Wonderful. That conjured up thoughts I haven't had in years!! Ugh!

11

"Well, well the prodigal son returns." I hear Aiden say when I step into mom's heavily populated dining room. Good grief here we go.

"Hey everyone. How're ya'll doin?" I put on my best smile and try to keep it together in front of those most dear to me.

"Good to see you home for a while big brother. We've missed you." Audrey says as she comes up for a hug. The little baby in her arms makes it a bit awkward but still feels good.

"I've missed you all too. You've all grown up on me. Now you're all married with children." I run my hand along Baby Abbott's cheek.

"Almost all of us. Austin get on that would ya?" Aiden says and smacks Austin on the back. These two are like oil and water. Still after all these years.

I have missed them and this place. Who knew?

"Not for lack of trying." Austin says and gets elbowed in the side from Leah which makes him shrug his shoulders. "Well it's true."

"Yes it is. I've been with them enough that it gets hard to breathe with all the sexual energy in the house."

"Oh shut up! You can all rest assured that I'm pregnant. Can we change the subject now?" Leah says and buries her face in Austin's chest.

"Leah? Why didn't you tell me that?" Austin says and lifts her head up to look at him.

"I was going to surprise you tonight but this dinner changed our plans a little." She smiles at me.

"Princess I couldn't be happier. I love you so much." Austin says and kisses his expecting wife.

"We are all so happy for you two." Ma says and hugs them both.

"Thank you. I really didn't want to spill the beans like this but ya'll really didn't give me a choice." Poor Leah looks so uncomfortable.

"Ok moving on, do you all remember Amie from the wedding reception? She's helping plan the church conference. She is a God send." My Mom steps up in front of us and says.

"That she is. She's going to let me room with her in the apartment while I figure out my next move."

"She is?" Mom shrieks out in disbelief. I can see the shock and anger filling up Amie's eyes as she shoots daggers my way. I know this was the only way to get her to agree with my roommate idea.

"Are you sure about this Amie? Aaron has a room here at the house." She puts her arm around Amie and glares at me too.

"Oh it's no big deal. There's plenty of room and it's your apartment anyway." She plasters on a big smile that can't be real. I'm gonna get it later that's for sure. I'll never stop hearing about it either. From she or my mother.

***

"You're used to getting your way aren't you?" I ask Aaron the first chance I get. I am very annoyed with this man. He didn't even give me a chance to think about it. Jerk.

"Normally, yes. I knew you would agree eventually. I just hurried it along." He smiles. Of course he does.

"You're a jerk. I'm going to regret this aren't I?" I glare at the world's biggest pain in the butt.

"Regret? Never. Enjoy? Very much." This time he smiles and winks before walking over to his dad. Grrr!

"He can be quite the pain. Nice to know he hasn't changed much in that regard." I hear Audrey step up beside me and say. We're both watching Aaron across the room. She busted me watching her big brother. Great!

"That he can. How is married life and mommy-hood?" I ask trying to distract her from my gawking at Aaron.

"Amazing! Things couldn't be better. So, you like my brother?" She smiles and I about faint. How do I respond to that?

"He's a nice guy but a lot to handle."

"Not what I meant but okay."

"Oh not like that no. We are friends I guess, you'd say. Nothing more than roommates." Such a liar.

"If you say so. Just be careful. He's got a lot of secrets right now. He won't even tell his siblings."

"He will in time. Don't take it personal. And don't worry, we are just friends."

"I'm worried about you not him. He's a big boy. You seem like a wonderful person and I would hate to know my brother hurt you."

"Thanks but I'll be fine. If you'll excuse me I need to run a few things by your mother. Nice talking to you." And I scurry away. That girl has no idea what I've been through. There's nothing Aaron could do that's worse than that. Well, we're only friends anyway no need to think about it. If only my body didn't respond every single time he looks at me. I think I'll sneak out and go home and to bed before my "roommate" comes home. I don't think I can deal with him any more tonight.

And that I do before anyone can realize I'm escaping. Especially Aaron.

***

"Well everyone thanks for giving me the time to figure things out and not hound me for info." I say as everyone starts to get ready for home.

"We love you Aaron and we know you'll tell us when you're ready." Audrey gives me a hug before grabbing baby Abbott from Maysen and heading out the door.

"Talk to you all later. I'll see you tomorrow Mom, Dad." I give hugs and head for the apartment above the garage. I'm worn out from all the family being here but also a bit excited for what I'm going home to. And whom. I remember the fire in Amie's eyes when I told everyone I was rooming with her and it makes my heart rate speed up.

I open the front door and am instantly disappointed to see there are no lights on anywhere inside. I know she left at least thirty minutes before I did. She must have gone straight to bed. I was really looking forward to getting into another heated conversation with her. Chicken.

I get a beer from the fridge and walk out onto the balcony to sit and relax from all the night's excitement. I'm so thankful no one pushed me to spill the beans. I'm not ready to tell all of them but I guess Mom or Dad could tell them. Wonder if they would so I don't have to. Or I could tell Austin, he would tell everyone. Mental note to tell him tomorrow.

***

Laying here in bed I know I heard Aaron come in earlier and go out on the balcony with a beer. I hope he's doing okay with all the family pressures about what's going on. I really should go out there and keep him company. I could use a beer. But is it wise for me to go out there? I can't keep my hormones in check around him for some reason.

Dang it! I can't stop feeling guilty for not checking on him. I groan and roll out of bed. Stopping in front of the full length mirror I see I'm not dressed too risqué to go out there. A t-shirt and boxer shorts. Here goes, I know I'm going to regret this. Ugh!

I grab a beer from the fridge and see he's still out there with his head leaned back on the chair. I breathe in deep and slowly let it out as I walk out the door and towards him.

"I thought you were asleep." He says before I get all the way out the door.

"I couldn't sleep. Why aren't you sleeping?"

"You were hiding from me and I'm not sleepy." He says with a slow smile as I sit across from him.

"I wasn't hiding. I was exhausted when I left dinner but when I tried to sleep it didn't happen."

"You still mad at me?"

"No. I was going to say yes anyway."

"See, I told you. How did you get so close to my Mom?"

"I did your brother's reception and we really hit it off. So when she asked me to help with the conference I was excited to do it."

"She really likes you."

"I like her too."

"I like you too." He looks surprised by that realization.

"Why do you look so surprised? I think I'm a pretty likeable person." I kind of felt offended by his surprised expression.

"I've never taken to someone so quickly. Last time I did I got burned." I can see the demons he's got buried in his eyes. Poor guy. There might be more to him than that handsome face and smile after all.

"What do you mean? I'm sorry, that's none of my business."

"No it's okay. I just don't talk to anyone about my personal life so no one ever knows what's going on with me. Except for my secretary Monica."

"Is she the girl who broke your heart?"

"Broke my heart? No. Piss me off? Yes. But no it wasn't Monica. She's like my little sister."

"Ah, so who was she then? This girlfriend that made you so bitter towards women?"

"Wife. She was my wife."

"You were married? Does your mom know that? She told me you were the last one that hadn't been."

"No, no one in my family knows. From the look on your face I can tell you think even lower of me."

"No you are so confusing. I don't understand you, that's all. Not my place to judge."

"Payton and I had a quickie wedding in Vegas and it ended as fast as it began. I just never had the chance to tell my family. And who wants to tell them they got married and divorced in the same sentence?"

"I'm sorry. No wonder you're the way you are and don't come home. You have to deal with stuff and it all becomes real here."

"Exactly. You're the only one to ever get that."

"If you don't talk about it then it can be forgotten."

"See, I knew I liked you for a reason. We're going to get along just fine."

"Roommates." And we clink our empty bottles together.

"I'll get us another round." He stands up to walk back inside and catches me looking at him from head to toe. I try to hide my embarrassment but he just smiles and walks inside.

***

She just checked me out. Maybe she's feeling these sparks between us too. Holy crap we might burn the house down.

Opening up the refrigerator door to get more beer bottles I can feel the cool air and consider climbing inside to cool off. I can't believe I just told her about Payton. I have diarrhea of the mouth when it comes to this girl and have the strongest urge to attack her and haul her off to my cave like some caveman. This pull and attraction is so powerful and has never happened to me before. I don't know how to handle it either. I don't want to seem like a player or like a jerk so I've got to keep my hands to myself. Hard as that might be.

"What took you so long? Thought maybe you went to bed without getting those beers." She smiles and my stomach ties in knots. That sounds so girlie. Idiot.

"Nah, used the restroom. Impatient are we? Or did you miss me?"

"You wish." She takes the beer from me and takes a long swig. That is the hottest thing I've ever seen a woman do. Down boy.

I clear my throat and say, "So what's your story? Enough about me."

"Let's not go there. I haven't had enough beer for that."

"I know where dad's liquor cabinet key is." I smile mischievously.

"Maybe after the beer's gone."

"After? Are we pulling an all-nighter?"

"I'm game if you're game."

12

A few hours and a lot of beer later, we've covered every subject but my life or any deeper into his. I'm about out of subjects to change to.

"Okay, enough stalling. What's your story Miss Amie the Party Planner?"

"I thought you had forgotten."

"No way. I told you about Payton. Now I wanna know a secret not everyone knows about you."

"I'm not from here originally."

"That I already knew. Stop stalling."

"You're going to make me do this now? Here?"

"Where else? Pillow talk?" And he lifts his eyebrows up and down.

"Unbelievable. You're something else you know that?"

"Yes ma'am I'm one in a million. You just haven't seen all of me yet."

"Oh I beg to differ. Remember the bathroom scene earlier today?"

"I meant inside you pervert. Get your mind out of the gutter!"

"Ya right. You meant exactly what I said."

"You're stalling again Amie."

"Aaron if I tell you will you promise not to blab it to your mother or anyone else?"

"Scout's honor."

"Were you even a Boy Scout?"

He smiles that mischievous smile and I know my answer.

"I still won't tell anyone. You can trust me."

"Ahhh I'm going to need something a lot stronger than beer for this conversation!" And he heads off to get the hard stuff. Good grief why am I planning on telling this man all about my past? I should just go to bed and forget this night ever happened.

Before I can get my mind made up he comes back with glasses and what looks like some kind of whiskey.

"This work?" He smiles and winks at me.

"I sure hope so." And I begin to tell him my story as he put it earlier. He sits completely quiet throughout.

***

This poor girl has been through Hell and back. I'm at a loss for words. How do I comfort someone who clearly hates being pitied? My heart goes out to her for sure while trying to keep a neutral expression.

"Wow, no wonder you don't like to talk about it. That's quite a story." I smile and wait for her to look up at me instead of the delicate hands she's wringing in her lap.

"That's why we needed the strong stuff. Feel sorry for me now?" She looks up at me finally but has a challenge in her eyes. She's waiting to see how I'm going to react.

"I'm sorry you were hurt so badly, yes, but pity you? No. What we go through in life is what defines who we are. I think you've overcome the worst and are working towards the best. You're a strong and intelligent woman who deserves everything she desires out of life." I pour us both another glass and hand her hers. I don't let go until she looks up at me, really looks at me. Once she does, I can see the sparks flying in her eyes and the awareness on her face.

"Thank you Aaron. I think you're the first person I've told that whole story to. I can't believe I did tell you all of that. Please don't tell anyone else, especially your mom. I don't want her to pity me."

"I won't. I would never do that to you. Your story is safe with me. You can trust me." I look at my hands and realize I've got her hand in mine too, not just her glass.

"I feel like I can trust you. Thank you." And she takes her glass and soft hand out of mine.

Disappointment. At the retreat of her touch, that's all I feel.

"You know what we need? Music. Be right back." I rush inside and get my phone so I can play music.

"Music sounds great." I hear her say when I return. She smiles at me with an almost nervous look on her face.

"A little country okay with you?"

"Perfect. Would you dance with me Aaron?" I turn to her in shock to find her with hands extended. I did hear her right.

"Of course, I was going to ask you anyway." I take her hands and pull her into my arms.

Wow this feels amazing. I can't help but sigh with the contentment I feel coming over me with Amie this close to me. She's so soft where I'm not and seems to have been made to fit here in my arms. I could hold her like this forever.

Forever? Whoa man where did that come from?

"This feels so nice, thank you. It's been a very long time since I've felt safe and trusted someone." With that comment she lays her head on my chest and I feel her body sigh and relax against me.

But this closeness isn't relaxing my body. This amazing woman does something to me and I'm powerless to stop these thoughts and feelings. I pull her even closer and now we are as close as allowed with clothes on and I can't help but wish it was closer still.

***

Being in Aaron's arms feels so good and I can't help but lay my head on his chest. I can hear his heart beating so fast. He's affected by me and being so close. Good to know it's not just me feeling the sparks and chemistry between us. I'm about to catch fire and burn to a crisp here. This man's touch lights a fire inside me that I didn't know exists. The more I'm around him the more I'm losing the self-control I've worked so hard to find.

I feel Aaron's hand traveling all over my back sending chills through me. My heart is racing and my breaths are coming quicker and quicker. When I feel as if I'm going to explode, I lift my head to look up at his gorgeous face and see the passion and desire burning in his eyes.

His eyes drop to my lips which seem to have a mind of their own as my tongue comes out and wets them. It's in that moment that I see his head bend down closer to my own and wets his lips. I inhale a quick breath right before his beautiful lips touch mine. And I thought there were sparks between us before? 4th of July fireworks is more like it. If anyone were standing here they would have a grand show of colors emitting from us.

Aaron slides his hands down my back and this time onto my bottom which he uses to pull me even closer. Now I can easily feel how kissing me has excited him. I gasp which allows him entrance into my mouth to take the kiss even deeper. I'm going to implode!

***

The taste of Amie's mouth and the feel of her body against mine has driven me past any sense of control. This is the most intoxicating woman I've ever met.

I slowly slide my hands up under her shirt where I'm greeted by soft velvety skin. This woman is incredible. I hear her moan into my mouth and know she feels the same way I do.

I end the kiss and look into her passion filled eyes and know instantly that this is going to happen. Oh yes it is. I lift Amie's shirt over her head where I find that she's not wearing a bra. How did I not notice that before? Oh my goodness what have I done to deserve this? I didn't think my heart could beat any faster but it definitely is.

"You are so beautiful Amie. I'm not sure I can take much more of this without carrying you to a bedroom."

"What's stopping you? Your bed or mine?"

"Your bed's bigger." I smile and pick Amie's legs up and wrap them around my waist. As I do she starts to kiss down the right side of my neck and my ear. Holy smokes I'm not sure I can get this to the bedroom without my senses going haywire!

"You are so hot Aaron. I can't wait much longer hurry up." And she bites down on my ear lobe making my feet move at warped speed to get her to the bed. No more messing around.

13

"Amie dear? Are you awake in there? I brought you breakfast. I need to go over a few changes the committee has come up with. Amie?"

knock knock

I sit up so fast in bed I realize I took a heavy arm and leg with me. Aaron. Oh my goodness he's still in my bed. And his mother is in my apartment right outside the bedroom door. Holy crap!

"Aaron! Wake up! Your mom's outside the bedroom door! She can't know about this! Wake up!" I hit him trying to wake him up as quietly as I can.

"My mother? Holy crap I'm glad I shut that door last night. She can't find me in here. She'll think I took advantage of you and never forgive me. And THAT I did not do." He smiles and kisses my bare arm. I look down to watch but realize that in my haste to sit up I didn't take the sheet with me and I'm sitting here completely nude. And Aaron is enjoying the view.

I roll my eyes and push him off the bed. He makes a loud thump but I hear him laughing which makes me laugh too.

I shush him and yell to his mom, "Be right out Amelia. I was in the shower!"

"Get in the bathroom while I change and go out there to distract YOUR mother."

"I can't watch?" He snickers and walks into the master bathroom fully aware of me watching him move about with nothing on but his wicked grin.

***

My mother knows how to interrupt at the worst time. I was hoping to have a repeat performance from last night before going back to my room. Thanks Mom.

I've been dressed in last night's clothes sitting on the side of Amie's bathtub for twenty minutes. I guess Mom decided to have the meeting in the kitchen here. Great. I have to get out of here but how do I do that without Mom seeing me. I would hate for her to see me come out of Amie's bedroom and get the wrong idea about us. She would start planning the wedding as soon as she got back to her house. Not happening.

I open the bathroom window and see the roof to the car port is about three feet below so I decide that's my only escape. I jump out the window and climb down the trellis. Once my feet hit the ground I'm startled to find my father standing there watching my great escape. He does not look pleased.

"Your mother is going to tan your hide young man."

"I know. I'm trying to keep her from seeing me. Please don't tell her she would get the wrong idea about this."

"Wrong idea? A man climbing out of Amie's bathroom window in what looks like last night's clothes? What idea should she get?" Ok maybe he isn't unhappy with me now that he's smiling like a cat that got the canary.

I frown and say, "I'm not my brothers. Happily ever after doesn't include me. Mom will never understand that and this won't help."

"Alright I won't tell her but if she asks I won't lie."

"Deal. Thanks Dad." I walk towards the front door of the apartment. It'll look like I've been out all night instead of up all night in Amie's bed.

As I open the door I see Mom and Amie turn to look at me. Mom does a once over and frowns when she realizes what I have on. Amie just smiles and blushes.

"Morning ladies. I'm just going to shower. Carry on." I smile at my mother but when she looks away I wink at Amie making her blush deepen. I slip into the spare bedroom feeling like a total jerk for disappointing my mom again. Oh well I am who I am. And being married with kids like my siblings is not me. Not even close.

***

Oh my… The look on Amelia's face when she realized Aaron had on the same clothes as dinner and coming in the front door looking like he'd had one wild night out. Poor thing. If only she knew where he had been all night. In my bed. But how in the world did he get out of the bathroom? A smile crosses my lips as I picture him climbing out the window like a teenager sneaking out to a party.

"You look happy today. Good to see you smile." I shake myself out of the Aaron dream I was having and look at Amelia.

"Oh! Um I was just thinking about how beautiful this room is going to be with the new flowers."

"Uh huh. You have that love look on your face. Think you've found a special man to settle down with?"

"Oh no. Marriage is not for me. I'm happy just as I am."

"Uh huh if you say so." Amelia smiles and we move on. But I know she won't let this go. I'm having a hard enough time keeping my mind on this meeting and not Aaron sneaking out of my window.

***

"Hey Dad. Think you can put me to work while I'm here? I could use the distraction."

"Distraction from your lady friend or life in general?"

"Dad, I told you I don't do fairy tales. I have so much going on in my head that she's the least of my worries." I lie. I don't want to think about her but I can't get her beautiful face out of my head. Manual labor is all I can think of to get her out. Lots of it. Bring it on.

"Aiden's been running the studs through the barns and I've been trying to help wherever I can. Austin really doesn't have time to come over and help much anymore since he got Stampley's. I could really use your help keeping things in shape."

"Like building fence or what?"

"That barn's starting to fall apart inside and out. The doors are all trying to come apart and I'd appreciate the help. You up for it?"

"Of course. I'll take the pickup into town and get the lumber and supplies. This will be great."

"Thanks son. Glad to have you back." He slaps me on the back and walks away. I have missed this man so much. Always so tough and strong but has the heart of a child. Loves as big as Texas.

I grab the keys off the hook inside the barn for the ranch pickup and head into town. As I'm about to reach the end of the driveway I meet an unfamiliar car entering. I slow to watch them pass and as I do I realize it's the beautiful woman I can't seem to get out of my head. My roommate. That was a smart idea you moron. Now you'll see her at all times of the day. And night.

I smile and wave while she does the same but I can tell she blushed a bit too. I wonder what's going through her head right now. Surely she isn't hearing wedding bells after last night? Oh good grief I hope not.

I have to keep my hands to myself. That's the only way to avoid the uncomfortable wedding talk. Never happening. I growl and turn onto the gravel road heading into Colvin. I will not let another woman control me. Never.

***

Oh my goodness I did not intend to run into Aaron again today. I was praying I could stay in town long enough that he'd be out of the house and busy doing God knows what. Of course I was wrong. Just when I was finally thinking of something other than him, his handsome smile appears and knocks me back on my butt. Ugh!

He smiled and I could have sworn he wanted to stop and talk to me. I do not want him getting attached. Oh goodness no. I can't have him thinking about rings and forevers when all I want is to enjoy being roommates with occasional benefits. I thought that's what Aaron wanted too but from the smile and happiness to see me, I'm not so sure anymore. How do I fix this now?

I have to keep my hands to myself. That's the only way to avoid the uncomfortable wedding talk. Never happening. I groan and pull up in front of the apartment still lecturing myself about letting a man get too attached to me.

"Hi there dear. How are you?" I startle to hear AJ say from behind me. "I didn't mean to startle you."

"Oh AJ hello. I didn't realize you were there."

"You seemed like you were having some inner battle. Everything okay?"

"Oh everything is fine. Thanks for your concern. Now if you'll excuse me I have a lot of work to do. Have a good evening."

"You coming to dinner tonight?"

"Um um probably not. I think I'll just eat in. Thank you."

AJ nods and finishes his walk to the main house. He can't possibly know why I don't want to have dinner with his wife and son right? No way. I think I played that cool too. He'll never know. And his wife will hopefully NEVER know either.

***

"Hey honey. I just ran into Amie out there in the driveway and she was a million miles away. Do you know what's going on with her? I asked if she were having dinner with us and she acted almost nervous to. Just weird I guess."

"Well AJ you know she didn't have anyone else around her when she came to stay here with us. Maybe our family gathering last night was just overwhelming to her. Did you tell her it would be just you and I along with Aaron? Well that is if he makes it. Did you know that young man came home this morning in the same clothes he had on last night. He stayed out partying all night. I think he's a little too old for that kind of thing don't you?"

"Yes dear he is. Are you sure he was out all night and just coming home?"

"Oh yes, I was having a meeting with Amie and he came walking in the front door and headed to the shower. That's just not acceptable. We need to get him something to keep him busy so he doesn't go down that path."

"Maybe we don't know all the story here honey. Don't go grounding your oldest son until you know the whole story. Now, should I go invite Amie again to dinner or leave her alone?"

"I'll call her. You go on and do whatever you were heading to do. I'll call that wild son of yours too."

"Wild one is he? He never was. He was always the hardest working one we had. Not sure he's resorted to being a wild child my dear. But whatever you say." AJ walks away smirking because he knows a bit more about this story but can't tell his wife just yet. She would go crazy and ruin the budding whatever this is between Aaron and Amie.

"Amie dear how are you? AJ says you might not be joining us for dinner tonight? Well I'm very sorry to hear that. I did want to let you know that it won't be the whole family this time and only the three of us and Aaron. We would have too much food if you didn't come. Oh okay well, you get to feeling better and we'll hopefully see you tomorrow night. Sleep well dear."

"Seems as she's got a bit of a migraine so she's staying in tonight. I wonder if I should take her something to eat."

"Amelia, let her be. She's an adult and she can take care of herself. She'll come to you if she needs something. Don't hover. You drive your own children crazy when you hover. I'm going to shower and get a little paper work done in the office. Call me when dinner's ready." He kisses his wife's cheek and heads off leaving her deep in thought. He's sure it's probably how to get Amie here without hog tying and dragging her. He chuckles and shakes his head. That woman is so full of love and compassion for anything she comes across. Aaron and Amie don't stand a chance against her. And I think they know it.

14

"Son, so glad you could join us for dinner tonight. Seems it's just us. Amie dear isn't feeling well so she's staying in."

"Isn't feeling well? I didn't know that. Maybe I should go check on her or take her a plate?" I say before I can keep the words from coming out. Mom gives me a puzzled look but Dad is sitting there with a smirk on his face. Oh brother. What have I done this time?

"She said she was fine son. No need to worry about your roommate. I'm sure she'll be good as new tomorrow after she gets some rest." Dad winks at me and I feel like a total fool.

"Aaron how are the repairs on the barn coming along? Your father says you're helping out around the 6AB. That's so nice to hear. Your father can do a lot but repairs like that? He's out of his league."

"Oh thanks dear. I could do them if I really wanted; I just hadn't gotten to them yet."

"It's okay Dad. Not everyone likes to do the repairs like that. I happen to like it so I'll get it all fixed up in no time. Good as new."

"You're such a good boy. Just wish you weren't going out partying all night and coming home in the same clothes the next morning."

"Amelia we talked about this. Leave the boy alone. He's an adult."

"Ma I'm sorry you saw that. Won't happen again, I promise." I look at dad again and he's raising an eyebrow at me. I hate that.

"It better not young man."

"Thanks for dinner Ma but I'm pooped and need some rest. Love you two very much." I give hugs to my parents and head out to the apartment. I freeze once I'm ready to go inside when I see the woman haunting my thoughts walking around in a sun dress and no shoes. Her feet are bare and bright pink polish on her toenails. She looks so happy and carefree. And sexy oh my goodness.

I stand out there for a minute and watch her realizing she doesn't look under the weather. She looks just fine. Now I'm curious as to why she turned my mother down for dinner. Hmmm.

"Well don't you look miraculously cured?"

"Aaron you scared the tar out of me again. You have got to quit sneaking up on me."

"Sorry. You were kinda in your own world there. Whatcha workin' on?" I walk closer and get a whiff of her. Clean scent with a hint of some type of flowers. It's her hair that smells heavenly.

"Is your Mom upset about my being absent for dinner?"

"Upset no. Concerned yes. She's worried you're coming down with something but you seem just fine to me. What gives?"

"Um nothing really I was feeling a bit run down earlier and felt a slight headache coming on but I soaked in a hot bath and feel 100% better."

"That's why your hair smells so good. Smells like the bouquets of flowers we always get for Ma."

"It does doesn't it? No wonder I loved them so much. And definitely the reason she does."

"I thought you were trying to hide from me."

"You? Um no. Just not up to dinner with your family."

"It wasn't everyone you know."

She shakes her head and I realize that she's nervous. Why would she be nervous? Oh my goodness she is having thoughts about us. Crap.

"Well, I need to hit the hay. Talk to you tomorrow." And I practically run to my room to hide. I can't let her get any ideas from my kindness. Ugh. Way to go moron. You're going to break this poor girl's heart and your mother is going to kill you.

***

What in the world just happened here? One minute we're talking and the next he's rushing off to his room. This man is so strange. He sounded almost disappointed that I didn't make it to dinner. He said my hair smelled good. He was almost ready to say something else to me then bolted. He couldn't have been thinking we were going to sleep together again could he? Oh brother.

I try to sleep myself but can't seem to get there. I've got so much going on inside this head between the conference and Aaron. Dangit I don't want to be thinking about him. Things never end well with me and love so I can't let it happen again.

I decide to go for a walk; maybe that will help me to sleep. I slip out of the apartment without making a sound and walk towards the corrals.

Once I get to the closest one I see a white horse come trotting up to me. She puts her head over the top railing and nudges me on the arm. I laugh and rub my hands over the sides of her head and nose. She's so soft and calm. What could she be thinking right now? Does she have man issues too? Man issues? I do not have man issues. Where did that come from?

"Hey girl. What are you doing up so late?"

"She wants to know the same thing about you." I hear from behind me. Aaron.

"Couldn't sleep that's all. What are you doing up? Thought you were tired."

"I heard you leave and was worried."

"Why? I'm a big girl and I can take care of myself. Have been for years."

"I know but I was afraid you were lonely. Are you? Is that why you didn't want to do dinner? Are you missing your own family?"

"No Aaron. It had nothing to do with family. Yours or mine."

"Okay. That's good to know. I guess I'll let you and Spook get to know each other. Good night."

"Aaron wait. I think I would like the company." That's the truth. I do like his company. We can be friends right? Of course we can.

"Okay well what about a drive?"

"That would be great. Where shall we go?"

"There's this special place on the ranch where everyone loves. Let's take the ranch pickup."

We drive for half an hour and pull up on what looks like the edge of the world to me but I see a small headstone and bench.

"Who's buried here?"

"No one actually. My sister in law Leah's little girl she lost is buried in New York but when she moved here my brother and parents helped make her somewhere she could go and talk to Shannon."

"That is the most wonderful thing I've ever heard someone do for another. How did she lose her little girl?"

Aaron tells me the heart wrenching story of what sent Leah back here to Oklahoma and I feel the tears forming in my eyes. How can one woman come back from so much tragedy?

"You and Leah would be good friends with what you've both overcame." I hear Aaron say sitting down next to me on the stone bench.

"Aaron I told you about my past but you promised not to tell anyone else."

"And I won't but Leah has been through her own Hell and I think she could really help you to get over yours."

"Maybe. This is a beautiful spot. You can see all the town's lights from here."

"You should see it in the day time. Heaven."

"I'll have to remember it's here. Thank you for showing it to me."

I stand to get a better view closer to the edge of the hill when I feel Aaron's hand wrap around my wrist.

"What are you doing?"

"Amie I have been thinking about you all day and I couldn't stop. I don't want to have a relationship right now but I enjoyed our night. How are you feeling?"

"I feel exactly the same Aaron. I was so worried you were into me and wanted more. That's the reason I didn't do dinner."

"I can understand that but you have nothing to worry about. Can we have an encore of last night though without our feelings getting in the way?"

"I thought you'd never ask. Take me back to the apartment please."

"Your wish is my command." He chuckles and we head back to the apartment both anticipating the feeling of each other.

"You better go in first or someone might get the wrong idea."

"Deal. See you in a bit roomie."

"I'll put the keys away and be right in."

15

"Good morning beautiful. You really are gorgeous you know that?" I say to Amie when I see her open her eyes and stretch.

"Morning. How can you be so chipper this early? What time is it anyway?"

"It's a little after six. I take it you're not a morning person?"

"Not if I can help it. I love to sleep in and stay up late."

"You definitely kept me up late last night." I kiss her lips and see her blush.

"You can't seriously think we're going to go for another round this early in the morning?"

"No?" I kiss her stomach and run my hands down her legs.

"Casanova, this girl wants to sleep. Go away until at least ten!"

"You wound me. But okay I'll go for a run and then make you some breakfast. Think you could wake up for that?"

"Mmmmm breakfast does sound wonderful. After a short nap. Go run. I'll be here dreaming of running." She pulls the covers up and rolls over laughing. My goodness she is so sexy. Just looking at her makes it tough for me to leave her here. I'd love to climb back under those covers and spend the day here with Amie but I do need to distance myself before it's too late. I could easily get used to waking up next to her and going to sleep each night after making love to her. I need to get blood pumping through my veins and not have thoughts of Amie naked and asleep in my head.

***

"Why does he have to be a morning person?" I growl and roll over pulling the sheet over my head. As I do I feel and hear my stomach growl in protest. "Ok maybe breakfast would be good."

I smile and roll out of bed but can't help think about last night. Falling asleep in Aaron's arms after so much passion. I could get used to that. Get used to having him wake me up with kisses every morning.

Whoa. Wait one darn minute Amie! You cannot get attached to this man. He is not here for your daily pleasure. Suddenly breakfast doesn't sound so good anymore. I can't let him think I expect him to make me breakfast after a wild night together. Oh crap!

I jump in the shower and get dressed as quick as possible praying that I'll finish before Aaron gets back from his run. I have to be gone when he does get back. In no way are either of us ready for what breakfast together can mean. No way.

I grab my keys and rush out the door to the car. Taking a quick glance around, I don't see Aaron anywhere so I climb in and put the car in reverse. I speed away from the ranch and towards town as quick as I possibly can. I'll just grab some breakfast at Sally's in town. That's a lot safer for my heart. And Aaron's. Nah he couldn't possibly think he has feelings starting for me. No. Just

98

because you're fighting it doesn't mean he's having the same trouble.

You idiot how could you let yourself start to fall for a man like Aaron. He's not planning on being here much longer and is as closed off emotionally as anyone would be in his situation. He doesn't want a relationship or children. Doesn't want the happily ever after.

Heck you don't either Amie. Where is this all coming from? Just enjoy your time with him while he's around and leave it at that. Easier said than done I guess. Great. I don't want to want someone again. Do I? What is wrong with me? I don't want to deal with the heartache that goes along with loving someone else ever again. My head needs to tell my heart and body that! Grrrr!

***

"Why did I tell her I would cook her breakfast? That sounds so domesticated. You idiot." I chastise myself as I run and the more worked up I get the faster I run. Before I know it I have gone much farther than I had planned to go. It's going to take me an hour to get home now.

I slow my pace and try to clear my head of anything Amie related. Just as I do get it cleared I see her car zoom by on the dirt road that leads to town.

"Well you scared her off you dummy. I guess breakfast is not needed." I chuckle and head back towards the ranch house. Mom will make me breakfast.

I walk into the main house to find it's quiet too. Where is everyone? I was so sure they would be having breakfast at this hour. I search all over and don't see anyone.

"Fine I'll go to town to eat then. Sally's will take care of me." After fetching the ranch pickup keys from the office I head off to town to eat at Sally's. "I'll just eat by myself then if no one else wants to."

As I drive up to Sally's and park I can see that familiar compact car sitting a few spots down. Great minds think alike because she's in here too. She fled eating my cooking to come get Sally's. Interesting. She obviously didn't have anything to do instead of eating with me. She must have panicked and left. Wonderful. Now she'll think I followed after her.

I walk into the café and look around to see who's inside until I reach the face I was actually looking for. Amie. Gosh she is so beautiful. My stomach does a flip flop but I just brush it off as hunger pangs. Yea right you dummy you know she does something to you that you don't want to admit. Dangit!

Once she looks up at me I just wave and sit down with my back to her. There. She can't think I was following her now.

"Hey handsome what can I get ya?"

"Hi Sally. Pancakes, bacon and scrambled eggs please. Oh and coffee. Thank you."

"Good to see you back in these parts Mister. Been too long."

"Yes it has. Good to be back." I say as Sally turns and heads to the back.

Waiting for my food I let my mind wander to last night. That happens so easily and often now.

***

"Hi Amie. Mind if I join you?" I look up to find Leah standing next to my table. I was so afraid it was going to be Aaron that I was trying to ignore them.

"Of course! How're you feeling?"

"This morning sickness is the worst!"

"It will be worth it someday right?"

"I sure pray so!" She laughs and sits down, "How do you like life on the ranch?"

"It's so peaceful and I surprisingly love that part of it."

"After being in New York it was a welcome break to have the silence of Colvin for me too."

"I can imagine. Everyone has been so nice too. Amelia's a God send."

"And Aaron."

"What about him?"

"Is he a welcome break and a God send too?" She says with a wicked grin on her face.

Oh brother. Here it comes.

"I really don't see much of him."

"He lives with you how do you not?"

"It's only been a couple of days. I really don't see him that much." I lie. Boy do I lie. If she only knew how much of Aaron I had been seeing.

"Uh huh. You're roomies but eat breakfast at the same cafe but at different tables? Seems weird to me. Have a fight over the big shower?" Another evil grin.

"No. He was gone on a run when I left this morning. I haven't even seen him today. Well except when he came in here."

"Well, Austin's over there with him we should go join him so you don't have to sit here alone." She stands and waits for me to follow.

I feel frozen in place and filled with dread. How do I go over there and face Aaron now? Especially with his family sitting with us. Awkward.

***

"Hey brother whatcha doin' here? I'm sure mom had breakfast ready this morning."

"When I came back from my run no one was around. So, I came to town. Wanna join me? Where's Leah?"

"She's over there with Amie. Why aren't you over there with her?"

"Why would I be? She's not my girlfriend or anything."

"Whoa. Testy testy big brother. Oh look the girls are coming to join us. My wife and your non-girlfriend that is." I wish I could punch that look off his face. Jerk.

I watch as Leah and Amie reach my table. Leah slides in joyfully next to Austin leaving next to me the only place for Amie to go. Wonderful. Well played universe, well played. I guess we're having breakfast together after all.

"Well scoot over moron so Amie can sit down." I glare at Austin and scoot over as close to the wall as I can get. Heck I would climb up the wall if it would keep Amie's body from touching mine at this point.

***

This is the most awkward situation. I tried to stay away from him but now I'm forced to sit next to him in this super small booth. If I scoot over any farther on my side I'm going to fall off and hit the floor. That would top this morning off.

"I was asking Amie how she liked living on the ranch. She found it a good change like I did." Leah says to break the awkward silence.

"It's great, yes. Your mom has been wonderful to me." I say to Austin with a shaky smile.

"Mom's the best. She would move Heaven and Earth to help someone. Even if they didn't really need the help. She has the uncanny ability to see the best in everyone she meets." Austin says with pride.

"You're biased. But also correct. She took a chance on me when it came to your reception and again for the conference. It's been great working with her."

"She likes you. She knew you would do a great job on both. If you stick around Colvin after the conference I bet you'll have jobs lined up all over." Leah says and squeezes my hand that I have sitting on top of the table.

"The conference is still a few weeks away so we'll see how that goes first before making any future decisions." I smile and feel relieved when Sally chose this moment to show up with our breakfast.

"Nice to see you joining this fine bunch of people for breakfast Amie. Much better than sitting alone." She winks and walks away.

"Aren't you two eating with us?" Aaron finally says something. I was beginning to wonder if he was mad at me for coming over here.

"Oh we got ours to go. Which it looks like is ready. We'll talk to you two later! You both should come over for dinner tonight!" Leah says and hops up pulling Austin with her.

"I thought that was the reason you brought me over here. " I say puzzled.

"I just didn't want you two eating alone. You are roomies. Use this time to get to know each other better. Since you don't see each other much this is a great time to talk." Leah smiles that evil grin again.

"Goodbye Leah. We'll take it from here thanks." Aaron says in a stern voice and a frown. Leah just smiles again and walks away.

"Um I think I'll go back to my booth. Sorry to bother you." I start to get up but I freeze when I feel Aaron's hand on my arm.

"No you can stay. I really don't mind."

So I sit. But on the other side of the booth this time.

***

Damned Leah and Austin. They're in matchmaker mode already. And there's no stopping them. Before long my entire family will be following suit. Wonderful.

"I'm sorry about my brother and sister-in-law. For some off reason they're trying to set us up." I believe I turned a slight shade of red with that comment. I pray Amie didn't notice.

"It's okay. I just don't want to intrude on your breakfast."

"You mean since you slipped out on the one I was going to make for you?"

"Aaron I'm sorry. I didn't want you to think that after last night I expected you to cook breakfast for me like we're a couple."

"I honestly just wanted to do something nice for you. It didn't mean anything."

"I should have asked before leaving, for that I'm sorry."

"Water under the bridge. Last night was amazing by the way."

"I agree it was. I wouldn't mind a repeat of that performance every night." I see her blush. "Well while we're roommates that is."

"I know what you mean. Now eat up. You're going to need your strength."

16

"Amie, everything looks wonderful. I'm very pleased with how it all came together. You have been working tirelessly these past few weeks and that hard work has definitely paid off."

"Amelia I have to admit that I enjoyed every minute of it. Thank you for giving me this opportunity. I appreciate it more than you know." I lean over and hug this angel of a woman.

I've spent the last couple of weeks working on this conference during the day and spending every night with Aaron. Now that I'm done with the conference I'm really not sure where I go from here.

"Call if you have any issues. I'll be packing up my things."

"Packing? What on earth for?"

"Well, now that the conference is finished I thought you would want me to move out of the apartment."

"Goodness gracious no sweet girl. There are at least ten other jobs I have lined up for you. I just didn't want to overwhelm you so I was waiting until tomorrow to talk them over with you."

"Oh. Wow I never imagined I would be needed after this but I'm so grateful. I will wait to talk to you tomorrow."

***

"So, now that you've helped every old woman in town fix every little issue their house has, what are your plans for the future? I'm pretty sure being a handy man isn't exactly what you dreamed of." Aiden says to me while out on a horseback ride on the ranch.

"You know it's not what I dreamed of, but I screwed that dream up. I'm thinking it's time to start a new dream."

"And that would be?"

"You're the first one to ask me one of the tough questions that I know you're all thinking."

"Well everyone else is afraid to ask them in fear that you'll high tail it out of our lives again. We really have loved having you back big brother."

"I've had a few weeks to lick my wounds and figure things out. I'm all good now. Fire away."

"Amie has been good medicine has she?" He says with a smirk.

"It's been great spending time with her yes, but she's just as wounded as I am and until she figures her stuff out there's nothing else there for us. If that's what I wanted that is."

"Uh huh. You spend every waking moment that you're both not working together but you want me to believe that you don't want anything more than fun from her?"

"Yes. She was burned so badly the last time that she's not willing to start over. Those demons haunt her and until she deals with them she's off the market. Same as I am."

"What demons Aaron? Has she shared those with you?"

"Yes she has. I promised I wouldn't tell anyone else but I thought you might be able to help me help her."

"That sounds ominous. She's not going to like our help is she?"

"Not at first no but in the end she'll see why we did it and it'll actually help her move on. She'll be able to be happy again."

"Happy with you?"

"Who knows what's down the road. Will you help me or not Aiden?"

"Good grief I'm going to regret this aren't I? Why don't you ask my wife or Leah or your sister? Why me?"

"You're good at finding people. You found Karlie when she left you and look how that ended up."

"I went to her apartment Aaron, not some remote location where she was kidnapped or anything. You make it sound so heroic but I honestly just asked her mom for the address."

"Yes but you know people that could help too. Right?"

"No. Your sister in law Leah would help much better with that."

"I don't want her worrying about this while she's pregnant. Austin says she stresses about simple flower colors so this might throw her over the edge."

"Oh good grief I'll help. Who are we looking for?"

***

"Hey handsome."

"How did the conference turn out? Did the napkins and silverware behave for you?"

"Everything went smoothly you dork." As Aaron pulls me into his arms I feel as if this is the life I'm supposed to be living. That is until my brain gets ahold of that information.

Don't get too comfortable. Happily ever after is not you.

"Glad things went well. Everyone was pleased? Why am I asking that? Of course they were."

"Thanks for the vote of confidence but yes everyone was happy. Your mom especially. She wants to talk to me tomorrow about other projects she wants me for."

"That's great. Isn't it? Why do you not look happy about that?"

"I really hadn't thought about what the future entailed for me. I guess I thought once the conference was over I would move onto the next place and next job. But actually being able to stay in this amazing apartment and amazing town sounds so promising."

"Amazing apartment and amazing town huh? What about the amazing company you keep each night and sometimes in the morning?" He says as he whispers in my ear then biting my ear lobe.

"Well, I wouldn't describe that as amazing." I say and pull away from him, run to the bedroom and squeal, "It would be much better than amazing!!"

***

Lying here with Amie in my arms feels so right. Should I start another company here and try to build a life? Or go back to the big city and start another one there? Decisions.

"Penny for your thoughts."

"Hey beautiful I thought you were asleep." I kiss her forehead and see her smile while sighing deep.

"I was but I could hear those gears in your brain grinding."

"Just thinking about what I should do about my job. Should I build another construction company here or go back and start over there?"

"What feels right to you? Can you see yourself leaving here again or can you see yourself leaving happily? It's all about what's in your heart Aaron."

"I'm torn. I had such a good life before but that's gone. I love being in Colvin again whether I thought that could ever happen again or not. I just don't know. I don't want to do the wrong thing again. Me being an idiot got me into this place."

"True. But you also came home where you belonged and healed. Now you just need to find where you belong now as the new Aaron Blake."

"Belong. Hmmmm. I need to call Monica and see what she's got going on. She would be the best one to help decide. She's spent every moment connected to me since I hired her years ago."

"You two ever a couple or what? Should I be jealous?"

"No you have nothing to be jealous about. Wait? Jealous? Is this going a bit farther than just friends Miss Amie?"

"Maybe. It still scares the crap out of me but I like this feeling of being with you. Almost feels as if nothing could change it. Nothing could ruin it."

Oh boy. I know something that's going to ruin it. She's going to kill me after I tell her what I've done but how do I tell her. When Aiden and I started this search I honestly thought it was the best thing but now that I have to tell her about it I'm second guessing it.

"I need to tell you something and I'm not sure how you're going to react?" She sets up in a flash once she hears the tone of my voice.

"So you and Monica were a thing huh?"

"Oh my goodness no. Nothing about Monica. It's about you actually."

"Me? You're scaring me, spill it."

"I'm just going to come out and tell you. Please don't leave after we'll need to talk it out ok? Promise me?"

"No promises. Spill it dammit!"

"I contacted Brady's family. The Carlyle's. They're coming here on Saturday to talk to you. They have a lot they want to say to you."

"OH MY GOD WHAT HAVE YOU DONE?"

"Calm down Amie. They want to talk that's all. They're not mad anymore."

"They had no reason to be MAD in the first place. Aaron how could you? That is the one thing that hurts the most about back then. And you just stuck a knife right in and twisted it! Get out. GET OUT NOW! I don't want to ever see you again."

17

"I told you it wasn't a good idea. She's so mad at you now I'm not sure how you're going to get her to even look at you again."

"Aiden, I don't need to be reminded about how pissed off she is at me. I saw the look on her face and I heard the betrayal in her voice."

"She might see things differently once she talks to the Carlyle's. You never know. It probably was the best thing you could have done for her but it's going to take her some time to see that. Just keep moving yourself forward and things will turn out the way they're meant to."

"Getting sappy in your old age young brother. Marriage and fatherhood has been good to you."

"It has. Maybe one day you can experience both."

"I have done the marriage thing, never again."

"Oh yeah, forgot about the Ice Queen. What do you hear from Monica about the old business these days?"

"Not much since she quit a few weeks ago. I think she lasted three days. She's wanting me to start a new company here too so I'm thinking of having her fly in for a few days."

"Sounds like a plan. Another AB. Nice."

"Well, it won't be anything spectacular for a long time because I have zero dollars to invest. I'll need some help for sure, not sure where it will come from yet."

"Well, let me know if there is anything I can do to help."

"Thanks but I think all the big jobs that this town has lined up for me will be a start. Someone once told me that things will happen when and if they're meant to happen."

"That is one smart man who told you that. I better get home. Talk to you soon brother."

"Thanks again for everything Aiden. Tell everyone hello for me."

"You can stay at the house if you want instead of the main house you know."

"I do and thanks but Mom and Dad love having me here for a while. And I can keep an eye on Amie better than I could anywhere else."

"You've got it bad big brother. Just admit it." He says and walks out the door. Maybe he's right but I just can't let Amie know how I feel until I'm a success and she forgives me. The latter may never happen.

***

Today's the day that the Carlyle's are going to be in Colvin. I'm meeting them in town at Sally's and I really don't know that I can do it. How do I subject myself to their cruelty again? Damned

Aaron for making me do this. I'm never going to forgive him for this. Never.

I showered, blew my hair out until it hung perfect then drove myself to Sally's. That was twenty minutes ago and I'm still sitting in the car outside. I can see the Carlyle's sitting in a booth next to the window looking as cold and cruel as they did all those years ago. I can't make myself get out of the car. I don't understand how Aaron thought this would help me move on. I haven't felt this terrible since the moment Brady died and they said those things to me. How could Aaron betray me too? I was so stupid.

"Are you going to get out or sit here all day?" I jump and hear a female voice from outside my window. I know who it is before I even turn to look at her face. Or should I say their faces?

"Amelia, Karlie, Leah and Audrey. What are you all doing here?"

"We're here to give you support. Aaron and Aiden told us at breakfast this morning. Obviously you need that support at the moment." Amelia smiles.

"I do, thank you. I just can't make myself get out and go in there. Looking at them from here I can see the cold and unfriendly way they are. I can't go sit down with them again. I can't take their cruelty. Once in a lifetime is enough."

"You don't even know what they're going to say Amie. We all know you're upset with Aaron for contacting them but they wouldn't have come all this way just to yell at you again after all these years would they?" Audrey, always the word of reason.

"Probably not but just the sight of them makes me want to run away crying like a little child."

"You don't have to do this if you really don't want to. We can call Aaron and make him come take care of it since he's the one that started it."

"Would you? I thought I was strong enough to meet with them, but I'm clearly not since I'm still sitting in my car." I look down ashamed of myself. I don't like being weak especially in front of the world's strongest women.

"I'll call him right now. Why don't you come to the AK and we'll have some coffee, talk and just let you relax. Sound good?" Karlie asks.

"That sounds like Heaven right about now. I'll follow you there." I take a deep breath and one last look towards the couple awaiting my arrival inside that café. I'm not sure I'll ever look at Sally's the same from now on.

***

"What do you mean she wouldn't get out of the car? Did they see her? Oh goodness I've really done it haven't I? Thanks Karlie I'll head over there now. Bye."

You are the world's biggest idiot Aaron. You've done more damage than good and she's never going to forgive you.

I jump into a ranch pickup and race to town praying I can get there before the Carlyle's leave. They must think terrible things about Amie right now and I need to explain the situation. Ugh!

"Mr. & Mrs. Carlyle?" I ask and see the man and woman both nod yes.

"Hello I'm Aaron Blake. I'm the one that contacted you about Amie and set up this meeting today. This meeting that is clearly not going to happen. I apologize for her absence and false encouragement that she would be here. She actually didn't know I was contacting you and couldn't bring herself to come inside. She sat outside in her car for a half hour but couldn't do it once she saw you through the window. You really hurt her."

"Yes, we did. We were so terrible to her but we never meant to hurt her the way that we did. We were mourning the death of our son and lashed out at the wrong person. That we know and have been trying to find Amie ever since but couldn't seem to find an address that she was at longer than a few months. Then the trail went ice cold a couple months ago. That was until you called us."

"Yes, she had been sleeping in her car in the park here in town while she was planning parties during the day. My mother found her one night and offered her the upstairs apartment at our ranch. Amie doesn't know my mother found her though. She would be horrified."

"That poor child. This is all our fault. We took everything from her. Oh my goodness. What have we done?" Mrs. Carlyle starts to sob into her husband's shoulder.

These two don't seem cold and cruel like Amie had described.

"Why have you been trying to find Amie? You blamed Brady's death on her. What changed your mind?"

"Time and healing. We were so hurt when he died and lashed out at the wrong person. The shooter was the one we needed to lash out at but since Amie was closer and easier we chose her I guess. We have felt so terrible about that for so long. We were really praying we could make it right today."

"My wife and I were hoping to talk to Amie and apologize to her. We have spent a lot of money on PI's trying to find Amie. No one ever could."

"She hasn't had very much since she left your son's apartment. Their apartment."

"We kicked her out with nothing. We know. But we want to make it right."

"How do you plan to do that? Especially since she can't even face you again."

"We kept Brady's money in an account with a high interest rate and kept contributing to it over the years. It has a very sizable amount in it now. Close to four million."

"That's all good and well but what's Amie have to do with it?"

"It's in her name. She's the beneficiary of every cent."

"She's a millionaire sleeping in her car. Wow. I don't know what to say."

"Could you tell her for us and give her this letter from us? And the key to the lock box that has the information? It's in the New York State Bank and all hers." Mr. Carlyle hands me the envelope with a smile. He holds onto my hand a bit too long making aware that they are heartfelt words they're saying.

"I'll try but she isn't too happy with me because I contacted you without her knowing."

"You love her don't you?"

"Um well, I'm not sure about that yet. We've only been hanging out for a couple of weeks but I do care about her yes. That's why I wanted her to get closure with you two."

"I can't tell you how happy I am to know Amie found someone to love and protect her again after she lost Brady. We definitely didn't make life easy for her but God knew what he was doing and brought her here to Colvin to find you. Please take good care of her."

"If you happen to come with her to New York, please look us up and maybe we can have dinner. If she's ready of course."

"Wow thank you. Like I said I'll try. I can't even begin to tell you how shocked she is going to be. I'm in complete shock and it's not my money or life."

"Take good care of her. She deserves to be happy. She made Brady very happy but we didn't give her a chance. Make sure you give her that chance. Can you promise me that?"

"Yes ma'am. I promise. Thank you. Have a safe trip back home. And thank you for coming. She will appreciate it one day."

I get up shaking my head and try to decide if that really just happened or if I'm at home still sleeping. Looking down at the gray envelope in my hand proves that I'm not asleep. Now to find Amie and face her next.

18

"Aaron you shouldn't be here. She's very upset with you."

"I know Karlie believe me I know but I just took that meeting with the Carlyle's and there's something she needs to know. Something huge!"

"I still don't think she's up to it. I'll go see. You wait out here on the porch."

"Geez am I a stray dog now?"

"Act like a dog, get treated like one." She winks and smiles at me. Dammit I see why Aiden is so smitten. I just roll my eyes and shake my head. She really is something. A lot like Amie.

"What do you want now? Going to tell me my dead parents are here too and want to talk? Maybe Brady himself?"

I stand up startled by her voice. Wow she really is mad. There's anger dripping from her voice.

"Amie don't be ridiculous. I'm here because I met with the Carlyle's after you left and there's something you really need to know. Something huge."

"I don't think I want to hear this Aaron."

"Ok well they wanted me to give you this letter. I guess when you're ready to read it then you'll know all you need to know." I hand her the letter and turn to leave. "Goodbye Amie. Take care of yourself. I'm sorry I hurt you."

I walk to the ranch pick up and drive away. Why does this have to be so hard? I've walked away from women before. Heck I even walked away from a wife. This time it feels like my chest is going to split open. This sucks.

***

"Are you ok Amie?" Amelia joins me on the porch as Aaron drives away.

I turn and try to smile at her and say, "I don't think so. They wrote me a letter but I'm not even sure I want to read it."

"You can keep it and read it when you're ready. No rush. Come back inside and finish your tea."

"Thank you for being so kind to me even when your son is the one I'm so upset with."

"I'm not taking sides, just offering support where it's needed. Aaron is a big boy he can deal with this on his own. Besides his Daddy's gonna go talk to him when he gets home."

"I can't help but hope he's okay. I know I hurt him too but I feel so betrayed right now. Even if he did have the best of intentions, it still hurts."

"And it's going to hurt until you forgive and move on. It might always hurt a bit but it will get easier. Now that tea will help relax you for bed. I'll drop you off at home after you're finished."

"Thank you but I have my own car." I need to finish this tea and go curl up under my comforter for about a week.

"Ladies I can't begin to express my gratitude for your kindness today. You're the best friends a girl could hope for. Thank you so much. I'll see you soon I hope." I turn to walk away but am stopped by arms being thrown around me from all directions.

"We love you and are always here for you no matter what. We are all friends. You're welcome here anytime." Karlie says and the others second. I smile and walk to my car. Maybe this day isn't completely ruined. I finally feel like I belong somewhere. Except with Aaron. I thought we were moving in the right direction but I just can't believe he did this.

***

"What are you doing Aaron?" I hear my father ask from the door way to the study.

"Making sure she gets home okay."

"Who being Amie I take it?"

"Yes Dad. Amie. I really screwed things up and hurt her today."

"If it's meant to be it will be."

"That's where Aiden got that saying huh?"

"He stealing my lines again? That rat."

"I really did screw it all up. Badly."

"Sometimes we do things for the right reasons but it comes out all wrong. When that happens we're forced to wait around to see how things are going to fall. She'll be fine and so will you."

"Yes, but I'm not ready to say goodbye to her but I had to tonight."

"You don't want to be with her anymore?"

"Anymore? Who says we were together?"

"Son we aren't dumb or blind. You two were obvious by the way you looked at each other. Neither of you really came out of that apartment unless you had to. We're happy about you two being together. Two damaged souls finding peace with the other."

"Until I pushed too far. What do I do now?"

"Let her be. Let her decide what she wants. If she misses you and feels the same she'll come around. If not, you have to respect that."

"Thanks Dad. Oh there she is. Does she look like she's crying to you? Oh Dad I need to go to her."

He puts his hand on my arm stopping me, "No, you need to leave her alone until she's ready."

"That's going to be the toughest thing I'll ever do."

"Concentrate on Monica coming tomorrow and what you're going to start with another company or whatever."

"You're too wise old man." I hug him and walk to my room. Alone. I sure feel alone too.

***

"Does he love her as much as she loves him?"

"Yes my dear he does. Aaron has met his match and he's not sure what to do about it."

"That son of ours is stubborn and has for sure met his match."

"What's the big news he has for her from the Carlyle's?"

"He didn't tell you?"

"AJ would I be asking if I knew already?"

"No I guess not dear. We'll all learn the news when it's time I suppose."

"He gave her an envelope but I'm not sure she'll ever open it. She may just burn it without knowing its contents."

"That would be a shame. She may feel 100% better after reading it."

"I agree but it's up to her. These young adults are worse than when they were little kids running around catching frogs and rabbits."

"Yes my dear they are. But our grandbabies are just starting out."

19

I light a fire and sit on the couch in front of it sipping a cup of hot chocolate. I just got back from Karlie's and took a hot bubble bath to try and recover from the day's horrific events. Replaying things in my head I remember the envelope that Aaron gave me and the look on his face when he did. He wanted me to open it so badly but I couldn't. I turn my head to see the gray envelope still sitting on the kitchen counter. Taunting me. Part of me wants to run over there and rip it open. The other wants to grab it and throw it in the fireplace.

I stare at it for a good five minutes before getting up and retrieving it. Once I have it in my hands I'm not really sure what I had planned on doing with it. The envelope feels cold like the people whom had sent it for me. I have to admit that I'm a little curious as to what's inside but also terrified but I sit back down in front of the fire with it in my hands. I sit it on the coffee table and ponder what I should do with it.

I sit here never looking away from the envelope for about an hour before I feel my eyelids start to get heavy. I'll sleep on the decision. Maybe in the morning I will have a clearer head and be ready to deal with the envelope and its contents. Maybe.

A few hours later I awake with a jolt and realize that I'd been having a nightmare of the day that Brady died. I haven't had these nightmares for a very long time. Thanks to Aaron they're back. I try to relax back into my pillow but can't get my head to shut off or my eyes to close again.

The envelope. The sight of it pops into my head again and won't leave. It's the damned envelope. Fine, I'll go open it. I pull myself out of bed and walk to the living room. Yep, there it is still sitting on the coffee table. It looks innocent enough. Right? Geez I'm afraid of a piece of paper. Just open it and get it over with.

I slowly open the envelope and feel something hard inside it. I hadn't noticed it before but I never really held onto it too tightly before.

A key. Looks like a post office box key or something. I'm really curious now. I unfold the letter and see my hands shaking as I do. I take a deep breath and let it out as I focus on the words.

Amie,

We want to start out by saying we are so very sorry for the way we treated you when Brady passed away. Even when he was alive we never gave you the attention you deserved or the acceptance that he had craved of your relationship. We took Brady's death very hard and were distraught to learn we lost our only child. You were by no means the one we should have been taking it out on. You loved him too and he loved you.

We never wanted to believe that he could love someone more than he loved us. We were very wrong to think that. He would never have loved someone more, just differently and more passionately. His love for you was pure and his dreams for your future together were real. He wanted you to open your party planning business and he do the financial side of it. He wanted you two to become a team and live the happily ever after.

His time was cut short but you should never have been shoved aside and left alone with nothing to call your own like we did.

You were the rightful owner of everything just as much as Brady was. We are ashamed to say it took us years to realize that. We want nothing more than to make that up to you now. We're not sure if you're going to allow us to try, but we want nothing more than to do just that.

How you might ask? Well, when Brady passed away we put all of the money he had and the money from the sale of his assets into an account at the New York State Bank. We've also been making sizable contributions to it over the years along with having a large interest rate. There is close to four million dollars in that account Amie.

And it's all yours. We have you solely listed as the account holder and account beneficiary. The key enclosed is to the safety deposit box at the bank that has the paperwork in it that you'll need. Only you have access to this box. You can go whenever you're ready to do so.

We left you penniless and homeless all those years ago but we never want you to feel that way again. We have made sure that Brady will be able to help you reach your dreams. And his. We finally realized that his dreams were the same as yours. We whole heartedly want you to know how sincerely sorry we are for what we did back then and wish you nothing but the best in your future.

We also pray that you will one day find someone else to love and be loved by as much as Brady did. We will always be indebted to you for loving our son as much as you did and making him as happy as you did.

Good luck in your future,

The Carlyle's

Holy crap. I thought I was shaking before? I'm in disbelief now more than ever before. How can this be happening? Four million dollars? Mine? I have to sit down, there's no way to stay upright any longer. I wish Aaron were here with me. No wonder he wanted me to open the envelope so badly. They must have told him at the meeting. And I was so hateful to him knowing full well he was trying to help me.

I wonder if he's still awake. Most likely not and I'd wake up Amelia and AJ if I tried to get in now to talk to him. I'll catch him tomorrow. Tomorrow. Right now I really need to get some rest and hope to process this mess better tomorrow. Unbelievable for sure. What. A. Mess. Who's going to sleep after that?

20

"Well look at you stranger! You look so relaxed and happy. Being home must have been good for you?" Monica says as she rounds the corner at baggage claim the next morning.

"It's been better than I could have imagined. Not real sure what I've been running away from all these years." I hug my friend and ex-secretary. "You look like the Bahamas were good to you."

"It did after dealing with the she-devil. But that's all water under the bridge. What have you been up to mister?"

"I've actually been doing any handy man jobs around town and the ranch that I can. People are beating down the door to ask me for help. Which is why I wanted you to come and visit."

"You wanna start over with AB. I knew that was going to happen. We could go so big and make Payton wish she had never swindled you."

"No nothing like AB was before. I was thinking a local thing. Staying local." I can see the wheels turning in her head. Her face isn't telling if she's okay with the idea or hating it. "Seriously, nothing to say?"

"I'm thinking. Give me a second to process this bombshell. So you'd stay here in Small-town, Oklahoma and repair people's roofs for a living?"

"Not exactly. I actually have a long list of jobs that people want me to do. A new shop for my brother in law, a new nursery for my brother, new barns for my dad, etc. etc. etc."

"So it would be big jobs not just repairing a hinge on the gate type of things?" She says with her eyebrows drawn together.

"No, but I would help there if needed to. I have really enjoyed getting my hands dirty these past few weeks."

"Really? I guess when I first met you that's how you were. And where do I fit into this idea? You wanted me to come here for a reason." I shut the pickup door for her and run to the other side and get in.

"I want you to help me start it and get it going again like you did with AB. You helped me in more ways that I can explain. It wouldn't be anything like AB but it would be a new start."

"And you want me to move here to live with cows? Seriously?" Disgust. Complete disgust on her face.

"Yes. I can't do it without you Monica."

"Oh my goodness. Show me around and I'll answer you before my flight leaves in two days. Deal?"

"Deal. You're going to fall in love with Colvin and the 6AB Ranch. I promise."

"I'm going to hold you to that Aaron." And we ride the rest of the way to the ranch in silence as she takes in all the sights Oklahoma has to offer a big city girl.

***

I think I slept better last night than I ever have and had the most wonderful dream about Brady. He came to me and told me things were finally going to be okay. He gave me a kiss and a hug because he wasn't able to before he was killed. It was the sweetest thing I've ever experienced. Until I woke up I could have sworn it was real. It felt so real. I could even smell his cologne that he used to wear. I could feel the touch of his lips on mine and the sigh he made when we embraced. I wish it were real but it must have been my subconscious letting me know that it's time to move on. Funny how the one person I was so distraught from losing is the one to set me free.

I sit up in bed and look around slowly. A slow smile creeps over my face because I feel so comfortable in this apartment and for once it feels like home deep in my bones. I reach over for my cell phone and dial Amelia's number. "Good morning Amelia how are you today?"

"Well hello sweet girl. How are you? Hope you're better than yesterday. You sure sound better."

"I feel 150% better actually. Are you available for a chat?"

"Of course honey. Come on over."

"Let me get dressed and I'll be right over." I smile and spring out of bed like I were a whole new person gliding around my room and bathroom as if I were floating on air. I love feeling this happy and content.

After getting ready I step out the front door and see Aaron getting out of a ranch pickup and walking to the passenger side door and opening it. Who is that? He then reaches in the back and grabs a few expensive looking suitcases while urging his new lady friend up the walkway to the front door. Doesn't she look sophisticated?

Who in the world is that? Surely it isn't his ex-wife. She's about what I would expect her to be like.

I guess I'll wait to go and see Amelia, sure wouldn't want to get in the middle of that introduction. I wouldn't mind being a fly on the wall though when they all meet the infamous ex-wife. I can't believe Aaron brought her here after all she's put him through before and after their so-called marriage. His family is going to freak out. I think I'll read a book or watch TV and wait for the fireworks.

***

"Ma? Dad? Anyone here?" I say as I lead Monica into the main house. "Where is everyone?"

Then I hear Mom call from the kitchen. Should have known. "Aaron I'm in the kitchen. Dad's in town."

"Mom, there's someone I'd like you to meet. Mom this is Monica. She was my saving grace at AB."

"Well it's so nice to meet you Monica. I'm Amelia his mother. From what Aaron has told us you kept him on his toes. Something I'm grateful for." She gives Monica a great big hug making her have a panicked look on her face. Monica definitely isn't the touchy feely type.

I smile and say, "She's here to help me figure out what I'm going to do about another construction company."

"Oh well welcome to Colvin and the 6AB Ranch. Are you going to be staying with us here at the main house?"

"Yes she's going to stay in Audrey's old room. I'll take her now."

"Very nice to meet you Monica. Make sure Aaron takes you on a tour after you get all settled in." Mom gives Monica another hug but this time she hugs her back. I smile and Monica rolls her eyes.

"Nice to meet you too Amelia. Thank you for letting me stay here. It's a beautiful place." Monica grabs her bags before Mom can give her another hug or any type of physical contact.

"This way to your room." And we walk up the stairs away from the hug dispenser. I can't help but chuckle and shake my head.

Once we're out of earshot from my mother I say, "I thought you were going to melt from all those hugs you got. I know how you love to be touched."

She glares at me and slams the door to her room in my face. Audrey did that more times than I could count growing up. Feels good to have Monica and Audrey back in my life which feels like it's finally coming together. If only Amie would talk to me again.

21

I see Aaron and his devilish wife get in the ranch pickup and drive off so I think it's time to go talk to Amelia like I had planned on earlier today. I walk over to the main house and knock on the door. When Amelia answers she frowns at me.

"I'm sorry were you busy? I can come back later." I say and turn to walk away.

"No no no honey you're just fine. You need to quit knocking on this door though. You're like one of my children and I don't want you knocking like you're a stranger."

"That's what the frown was for huh?"

"I'm sorry if I was frowning. I was actually deep in thought too. Come on in. What did you need to talk to me about?" She leads us to the kitchen and sits down on a bar stool.

"I opened the letter."

"Oh honey I'm so glad you did. How do you feel about it?"

"Do you already know what was in it?"

"No. You don't have to tell me either if you don't want to."

"I want to tell you. There was a key to a safety deposit box at the New York State Bank in there along with an apology letter."

"How wonderful. I do hope you can find closure now for yourself. What's the safety deposit box for?"

"It has the paperwork needed for me to claim the very sizable account there solely in my name."

"That's wonderful. Did they set up a little account for you so that you're never sleeping in your car again?"

"What? You knew about that?" I jump up ready to bolt.

"Oh darling I never meant for you to know that. I saw you when I left the hospital when Audrey had the baby."

"That's why you gave me the apartment. I thought it was really a necessity for me to be here close by. I'm so stupid."

"Don't say that. It is very much a necessity having you close by. I was so glad I could offer you a solution. Now it sounds like you'll have a little cushion now."

"Not little no. Huge. Four million dollars huge."

"Oh my Heavens Amie that's beyond amazing. The Lord is providing closure where it's definitely needed."

"I just can't believe you knew I was living out of my car. I'm so embarrassed."

"Don't be. That's why I didn't want you to know. I didn't want you to feel bad. It's all in the past so let's not dwell on it."

"You're the most wonderful person I've ever met Amelia. I don't have a clue where I would be right now if it weren't for you."

"With money like that you're never going to have to worry about it again. Do you have to go to New York to claim it or what?"

"Yes, I was thinking I might go in a few days."

"I think that would be a great idea. Let me know if you need someone to go along with you. I'm sure Aaron would love to go with you too. He feels terrible for going behind your back and contacting the Carlyle's. You really should give him a chance to apologize."

"I'm sure now isn't a good time for him with his female company and all." I start to walk away knowing I can't have a conversation with his mother about this without getting upset.

"She leaves in a few days too. Maybe then you'll have forgiven him and allow him to go with you. Just think about it."

"I will thank you. Have a good rest of your day. I won't be around for dinner tonight." I give her a hug goodbye and slip out the front doors to the apartment. I need more time to think about this Aaron thing. His mother seems to think he's upset we're not talking but the way he was with the beauty from the big city makes me think that's not at all true.

***

"Ready for your tour ma'am?" I ask once Monica comes out of her room. I do a double take because she's not dressed in a suit with her hair up anymore. I think that's the only way I've seen her since I met her.

"What? Never seen a girl dressed in jeans on this ranch?"

"Never seen you look so relaxed. You're wearing boots and jeans with your hair down. Didn't know it was that long."

"Are you turning into a girl on me?"

"Ha no. Just a little taken back here. I'm sorry let's go." I usher her towards the barn where I've got horses saddled and ready to go.

"Oh horseback. Seriously? I don't think so cowboy. How about four wheelers? I can do those." She wrinkles her nose at me.

"Fine. I'll have them switch us out. City slicker think she can't handle a horse or what?" I smile.

"No you idiot I just don't want to die." And she storms off back to her room. This is going to be an interesting few days. Surely she won't be that uptight and scared or she'll never agree to moving here and helping.

Once the guys and I get two four wheelers ready for us I text Monica.

Ready City Slicker?

A few minutes later I see her come stomping down towards me. I smile knowing she's not enjoying herself yet but will love the view once we get out there.

"Which one do you want Miss?" I ask her before she climbs on the red one. I guess that leaves me the black one. Not that I care which one though, they're the same just different colors but as long as she thinks she got her way things will be much smoother.

"Follow me until we get out of the corrals."

"Can't wait. Let's go."

After we've ridden for about an hour we get to a spot where Audrey and Maysen want to build their house. I stop and turn to ask Monica a question to find she's already off the four wheeler and taking pictures.

"I didn't know you liked taking pictures."

"You never asked. Heck we never saw each other for anything other than work. I love to take pictures and these ones are going to be amazing. No wonder you like it here."

"True. I never did. I used to be so wrapped up in making money I never stopped to even ask the one person I saw and talked to every day what her life was like outside AB. I'm sorry about that Monica. I want you to know that this new company will be nothing like AB was. It will be all about helping where needed and not so much on being rich. I want to get back to helping those who need homes not those that need their fourth one."

"I get that. I just don't understand how you're going to get this going. There's going to be a lot of start-up costs."

"I've thought about that too. I'm going to meet with the bank next week and I'll see what we can do."

"You will need a partner won't you?"

"No I don't want anyone else worrying about funds. As long as I can pay the guys then that's all I will need."

"Guys? What about me?"

"Well you too of course. Does this mean you're leaning towards moving here and helping me again?"

"Do you have a crew? At least a few to start?"

"I have a few guys interested yes. I will also be helping wherever and whenever I can."

"Well, I think this is something I can get used to. Where do you live? Where do I live if I do come?"

"I was living in the apartment above the garage but, um well that's a story for another day. Right now I'm staying in the room across from you and you're welcome there as long as you want."

"And your parents are okay with this?"

"Of course. You met my mother. Amie calls her an angel which she really is. Now, are we really going to do this?"

"We'll need to make a business plan and get everything set up with the money before I can come back to stay for a while but I think so. And Aaron?"

"Yes?"

"Who's Amie?"

"Um she's the party planner working with my Mom."

"What's the story Aaron? I can tell there's more than just your mom's party planner. Let me guess she's living in the apartment above the garage and you broker her heart already so she kicked you out."

"You know me so well it's terrifying. Let's head back. I'll show you the rest of it."

"Let's go Casanova."

22

"Hi. I decided I'd come tonight after all. Is that okay or am I too late for you to add me?" I ask Amelia when she answers the phone. I saw Aaron and his wife leave on four wheelers so I'm sure they won't be back for dinner.

"Of course honey! We can't wait to see you. It will be ready in about an hour."

Now let's pray Aaron doesn't get back. I really don't want to have to sit at the same table as THAT woman. Grrr.

But the worst possible scenario happens the second I walk into the dining room of the main house an hour later. She's here. And so is Aaron. Together. Barf.

She looks even more beautiful than I had thought. I can't compete with that. No wonder he's stuck on her. But he told me she was toxic. What is she doing here then? And everyone seems so nice and happy she's here. How am I going to survive this dinner? Please don't sit me by her Amelia. Please.

"I'm going to sit you next to our guest Amie. Aaron will sit over here on this side." Damn she did it. Crap. I smile my best fake smile and take my seat. Also trying not to lock eyes with Aaron while I do.

"It's so great to have the three of you with us tonight. Dig in."

"Thank you so much for allowing me to stay in one of your spare rooms here on the ranch. It means so much to me." The she-devil says. I about choke on my bite of food.

She's staying in the house?? Oh my goodness. How in the world is this happening? She's the worst woman ever and she's staying in the house with Aaron?

I hurry through my meal and quietly excuse myself and thank Amelia and AJ for dinner. I claim that I have a headache coming on and need to rest. I say my goodbyes and head out the door as fast as I can. I have got to get away from these people. One person in particular. Grr!

***

I can see she's still mad at me. The lack of eye contact is a dead giveaway. I have tried to get her to talk but she's staying quiet. I really screwed up with her. I'm not sure I'll ever get her to forgive me let alone talk to me. Wonderful.

"Thank you for dinner. I'm going to go on home I feel a headache coming on and need to rest. Have a good rest of your evening." Amie says and rushes out the front door.

I look at my father and he just shakes his head no. He knows that I want nothing more than to run after her. Luckily Mom grabs my attention.

"Aaron she read the letter by the way. From the lack of conversation between you two tells me you didn't know that."

"No, I didn't know that. What did she say about it?"

"She wants to go to New York to get it all squared away. She's thinking day after tomorrow."

"That's the same day I'm leaving." Says Monica with a serious look on her face. I get the hint hush.

"You should go with her son."

"How? She won't even talk to me."

"You should go talk to her. You're the one who upset her to begin with. We're not doing it for you young man." Mom says and leaves the room to do the dinner dishes.

"You heard your Mother." And then Dad leaves also. Leaving me staring at a very inquisitive Monica.

"Your turn. What do you have to say about this subject? I know you're dying to put in your two cents worth."

"Yes I am. I've been keeping the questions to myself about her but I can't anymore. You're clearly in love with her. Why doesn't she know that? And why the heck is she mad at you?"

"I am not in love with Amie. I care about her yes, but no more than that."

"Uh huh. You look at her like you can't live without her. It's obvious you're in love with her you moron. Just admit it. You haven't ever felt like this about anyone else have you? Especially not the she-devil."

"How is it that you can read me so well? That just drives me crazy!"

"I've seen you with other women and you've never looked at them like you do that girl. Why is she mad at you anyway? What idiotic thing did you do?"

"Who says I did anything wrong?"

"Right. Just tell me what you did. I know you did something. She avoided you like the plague just now. I'm not sure she's too happy about me being here either but she at least tolerated me."

"Long story short I called someone that had hurt her and asked them to make it right with her. They came to meet her and she was furious with me."

"You did that without asking her first? No wonder she's mad at you stupid."

"I thought I was helping her move on. But clearly it made her the opposite."

"Clearly. Men are so clueless."

"What am I supposed to do Miss Know-it-all?"

"Go talk to her."

"She won't talk to me. You saw her avoiding eye contact with me let alone not speaking to me."

"Go up there right now and make her talk to you. Make her understand why you did what you did."

"She made it clear that she doesn't want to talk to me again. Dad says I need to just give her space and let her decide if she wants to talk to me again or not."

"Well, that decision is up to you. Do what you want. I'm going to my room to catch up on emails and make some calls. I'll see you tomorrow Casanova."

"You're a brat. Goodnight." I sigh deep and wonder what in the world I'm supposed to do about Amie. It's breaking my heart to know she's mad at me. Breaking my heart? Holy crap Monica's right. I do love Amie. This is not good; I didn't want this to happen. How did it happen anyway?

23

"Monica, it was great to have you here with us for a few days. You'll have a room here whenever you feel like coming back." My mom tells her when we're heading to the airport.

"Thank you Amelia. That's something I may need when I come back to help your son start a new company. Your hospitality is much appreciated."

"We always have room for friends of ours. Hurry back." She gives Monica a hug and a big smile.

"Okay, so do you have your ticket ready for New York Aaron?" I hear Dad say from behind us.

"No. Didn't know if I should follow her or not. She didn't even tell me about the letter or the trip."

"You're not going after her? Aaron my son, you have to follow her. I'll get you a ticket purchased and emailed to you as soon as you leave here. By the time you get to the airport in Tulsa the information will be ready. I can't believe you're not going on your own."

"Mom seriously. I'm not sure I need to go."

"Trust me you do. Here's your bag I packed for you too."

"You had this all planned out didn't you?"

"When you went on that site tour this morning I packed your stuff in case you decided to go."

"Alright I'll go but she's going to be upset with you when I show up there not me. I will tell her you're the one to blame." I smile and hug both parents. Taking the bag, Monica and I head for the airport. I pray Amie is okay with this and doesn't damage things even more. Am I going to regret this? Most likely. Ugh.

***

Today's the day I'm going to see the Carlyle's for the first time in years. I'm sitting on the plane waiting for take-off. There are a lot of people still boarding so I'm trying to calm my nerves. It feels like there's a circus going on in my stomach. My heart is racing like I've been running a marathon. My hands are shaking like I'm an addict needing my next fix. This is crazy. How can seeing two people again affect one person this much? How am I going to get through this? I wish Aaron were here with me. He'd know what to say to make me feel better. But you never told him about any of it, you idiot.

"Is this seat taken?" I look up and nod my head with a yes. As I do I'm blown away to see who is asking.

"Aaron? What are you doing here? How did you know I was here? Your mother. I should have known."

"I'm here to help Amie. Will you let me? I'm so sorry for contacting them behind your back and hurting you. Hurting you was the last thing I ever wanted to do."

"I know. I realize you were trying to do something good for me and I took it very wrong."

"It's true. I was trying to help you move on. I never ever wanted to hurt you though. Please say you forgive me."

"I do Aaron. I think I forgave you as soon as it happened. I was just scared of what that letter said and of the feelings I was having about them being here."

"I really am sorry Amie. It's been killing me that you didn't want anything to do with me."

"It's been just as hard for me. I've wanted to tell you so many things. I'm sorry too. Are you going to sit down or stand the whole flight?" I smile and reach for his hand. Once he sits down I throw my arms around him and start to feel so much better the instance his arms go around me.

I've fallen 100% in love with this untouchable man. Way to go Amie. How are you going to get out of this broken heart?

***

Amie and I talked the entire flight while never letting go of each other's hands. It feels so right to be sitting here with this amazing woman by my side. And talking to me again. That makes me smile.

"Where should we go first?" She asks me once we've gotten off the plane and hails a taxi.

"Let's go check into the hotel and then do dinner. We can save the nitty gritty stuff for tomorrow."

"Do you have a room reserved somewhere?" She asks and looks at me like she hadn't even thought about lodging.

"I'm sure Mom's got that covered too hold on." I take out my phone and check the emails from Mom. "Yep, we're set up at one on Madison Avenue."

"Aaron, I'm so glad you're here. I don't know why I didn't ask you to come. I have to say I'm happy your mom intervened." She lifts her head and kisses me straight on the lips. I can't help but pull her closer and pour all the feelings I have into the kiss.

"I have missed this so much." I moan into her mouth after finally coming up for air.

"Me too. Can dinner wait a while?" She smiles mischievously at me.

"It can. We have all night." I kiss her again before the cab pulls up to the hotel and we get out. I feel like such a lucky man to have this beautiful girl with her fingers intertwined with mine. My chest swells as I feel the pride rise inside. I smile and walk with my head held as high as I can towards the front desk.

***

"Good morning beautiful." I hear Aaron say beside me. I hold my breath for a second to make sure I'm awake and really did hear him say that. I open my eyes to find he's lying on his side staring right at me with a gigantic smile on his face.

"Good morning but I highly doubt I'm much of a sight this early." I groan and roll over. I get about half way over when I'm yanked back towards him.

"You are so beautiful it hurts me to look at you sometimes."

"Oh my goodness you don't have to say corny things to get me to like you anymore. After last night you should know how I feel Aaron." I shake my head and get out of bed. I've got to get my hair in some sort of order and brush my teeth. I bet my breath is horrible.

"I think I know how you feel but you haven't actually said it."

"You're just fishing for compliments now mister." I say and shut the bathroom door, stopping dead in my tracks at the sight in the mirror.

How can he think this is beautiful? It's dreadful. Ugh.

After some-what fixing myself in the bathroom I walk back out into the hotel room and see that Aaron has gotten up and made coffee. This wonderful man knows how to make coffee too? Be still my heart.

"You made coffee. Just what I needed. Thank you."

"Here you go. A cup just the way you like it." He kisses me then hands me the mug. I sigh and take a sip. This is the life. Coffee made by a handsome man each morning? Yes please!

***

"So, I thought we could do the bank thing this morning and then maybe meet the Carlyle's for a late lunch." I say to Amie once she's gotten dressed and ready for the day.

"Sounds fine. I'm very nervous though. I'm not sure what to expect or what to feel." She walks over to me and wraps her arms around my waist. Once she lays her head on my chest I kiss the top of her head and hug her tight.

"Whatever you feel, is the right way to feel. No one else has been through this but you. No one is judging either. Just relax and breathe."

"I think I'm ready. Let's go before I lose my nerve." I hear her say not sure if she's trying to convince me or herself.

"Let's get it over with so we have more time for sightseeing."

"Deal. Let's go." She takes my hand and out to face the bank we go.

24

"Ah, Miss Benjamin. So glad to finally meet you. Thank you for coming today. Right this way." The gentleman in the $500 suit held out one arm ushering us into a quite large room with a big table and many chairs. The wall of windows allowed the best view of the city I had seen yet.

"I'm sorry but how do you know who I am?"

"Oh I'm so sorry where are my manors? Mr. Carlyle called earlier in the week saying you would be in today and we've always had a picture of you on file. Your picture doesn't do you justice I assure you." He smiles kindly and looks back at his files.

I look at Aaron and he's looking at me too. It seems so strange to me that these people know me without ever actually meeting me. Aaron must feel the same by the look he's giving me.

"Thank you for meeting me today. What exactly do I need to do?" I set the key I was given on the desk and slide it over towards him.

"Well, first I'll go get your box for you and let you get inside of it. I'll be right back." And he scurries off to who knows where in the humongous place.

"This is weird. I feel so out of my element here and I've had quite a bit of money in banks like this before." He smiles and squeezes my hand for support.

Before long the gentleman returns with a small black box with a lock on the front. He sets it in front of me and says, "I'll leave you alone. Please let us know when you're ready."

"Ok thank you." I just sit there staring at the little black box. I haven't a clue what can be in here and I'm not so sure I want to find out. I look over at Aaron again and he smiles then rubs my back.

"Whenever you're ready Amie. There's no hurry." He leans down and kisses the top of my head.

I take a deep breath and let it out while reaching for the key. Inserting it into the lock I see that my hands are shaking again. I feel like I'm going to get sick.

"I can't do this Aaron. Will you open it please?" I take my hands off the key and lock so fast you'd think it burned me.

"Sure." He stands up and scoots the box closer to him and looks at me waiting for a nod. I do nod and he opens the box. He hesitates for a few seconds then lifts out a smaller red box. I recognize that box and gasp.

"That's Brady's box that always sat on his desk. Oh my goodness I really think I'm going to get sick now." I put my hand over my mouth and Aaron stares at me waiting for my next reaction.

"Do you want me to open it too?"

"No, can you hand it to me please?" He takes it out and sets it in my lap. I just sit staring at it like it's going to open itself.

"Do you want me to leave the room?"

"No it's fine." I run my hand over the lid of the box and finally lift the lid. Inside I see a single envelope and a small blue box. I take the envelope out and see my name written on it in Brady's handwriting. I can now feel tears start to pool in my eyes while I take the piece of paper of out of the envelope.

I take another deep breath and start to read.

Amie My Dearest,

For your birthday I wanted to get you flowers which I'm about to run out and get. In case you wake up before I get back I hope you're reading this. You're the most amazing woman I have ever met and I can't believe you're my fiancé. You have promised to marry me and love me until our last breaths. I want you to know that I will forever think of you as the mother of my children and the woman to stand by my side for the rest of our lives.

Happy birthday my love. I pray you're going to have the best day ever and love your present in the little blue box.

Love you forever,

Brady

As I finish the letter I feel tears running down my face. I put the paper back in the envelope and look at the last remaining box inside. It looks like a ring box but Brady had already proposed so it can't be that type of a ring inside.

I shakily lift it out of the red box and open it. I'm shocked to find that Brady had a ring inside with my birthstone and diamonds. It's absolutely gorgeous. With tear filled eyes I look up at Aaron to see he's trying very hard not to comfort me. I smile and stand up to hug him. As soon as his arms go around me I burst into violent sobs. He just rubs my back and kisses the top of my head. How did I get so lucky to have two wonderful men love me?

***

"Can you let them know we're ready?" Amie asks me when she's wiped her eyes and cleared the running makeup off of her face. The sight of her hurting just breaks my heart.

I smile and simply say, "Yes."

I walk to the door of the large room and motion to the nicely dressed man that we're ready. He rushes forward to join us again with a genuinely kind smile on his face.

"This really won't take much longer Miss Benjamin. There are papers that need your signature then you'll be all set." He opens the top file on his stack and shuffles through the paperwork. Once he finds the one he is looking for its scooted across the table to me with a shiny black pen on top. "Please sign at the X on these pages. This will finish the transfer of funds to your account here at the bank and you will then be authorized as the account holder. We do have a few accounts at other banks linked to this one so that it will automatically transfer for your convenience."

"How much are we talking in each one?" She asks unsure if she can handle the answer.

"There are eight banks in the vicinity that we have a close relationship with which each of them holds $500,000.00 exactly. Our bank here holds the remainder of the $4,000,000.00 left to you. The amount that we have here for you in our bank is for the interest accrual and payments the Carlyle's have added. Your balance with us currently is $385,462.19."

Amie gasps so loud both of us look at her. I can see her turn a little red and know how out of her element she is here. Both of us men know what it's like to have a lot of money but this is just unreal to her. She went from living in her car to now having over four million dollars at her disposal.

I think she's about to faint so I grab her just before she slides out of her seat.

"Can you give us another second? This is all just overwhelming to her." The man kindly leaves the room looking almost guilty for making Amie faint. I smile knowing she's taken such an important and serious man down to mush. She's good at that for sure.

***

"I'm so sorry about that. I don't know what happened. I'm so embarrassed." I say and cover my face with my hands.

"Don't be embarrassed. This is a lot for anyone to get thrown at them at once. You're no different." Aaron kisses me lightly and squeezes my hands.

"Are you ready to wrap this up Miss Benjamin?" I hear the gentleman say from the doorway.

"Yes please. I'm very sorry about that."

"It's quite alright. I do apologize for throwing it all at you at once. I just need you to sign this last page and we'll be all done."

"Thank you."

"Your debit card, checks and bank statements will start to go to your address in Colvin. If you are ever in need of anything, please give me a call at my private line here at the bank." And he hands me a business card. I feel so important but so childlike at the same time. This is so bizarre.

"Thank you so much for your assistance."

"Take care Miss Benjamin." And he walks out the door leaving me with the paperwork proving I will never have to worry about money again as long as I live and probably as long as my kids live. Kids? Whoa Amie. One step at a time.

"Can we go now?" I smile and take Aaron by the hand. I can't get out of this place fast enough. I need fresh air.

"Are you ready for the next meeting?" Aaron asks and I smile at him while he ushers us out the doors of the bank.

"I guess." He forces a smile and on we go to the next stop on this crazy ride.

"We don't have to go if you really don't want to."

"I know but I need to do it and get it over with once and for all."

"Let's go then." Aaron hails us a cab and tells the driver where to go. This is going to be interesting especially since I've never stepped foot in a country club in my life.

25

"We're here to meet Mr. & Mrs. Carlyle." I tell the hostess when we walk into the ritzy country club. Talk about being out of your element for Amie. I've been in them before and even a member at one but this poor girl's tied up in knots. She's hiding behind me like a whipped child as we follow the hostess into the dining room. Everyone's looking at us like we have three heads making it even more uncomfortable.

We follow the hostess for what seems like forever until she opens a set of French doors that open up to the outside patio. She points to the left and towards a couple sitting along the edge. Once the couple sees us coming they stand and smile at us.

By the looks on their faces I can tell they're just as nervous as Amie is. That makes me feel a little better and I wrap my arm around her waist and pull her to my side. I don't want them to think she's still broken by them. She's a strong and beautiful woman and I want them to see that after all these years.

I can feel her tense up as we reach the table and they shake my hand. Mrs. Carlyle rushes over and hugs Amie which makes her tense up even worse. I don't think she saw that coming but she smiles and looks at her feet.

"Please sit down. Let them sit down dear." Mr. Carlyle motions for us to sit across from them. He pulls out his wife's chair and pushes her in. I do the same with Amie hoping to look somewhat civilized.

"Amie we are so pleased to have you sitting in front of us." Mrs. Carlyle says with a monster sized smile. Her teeth are so white and perfect it's almost unnatural.

"Thank you for inviting us." Amie looks at me then answers. I smile hoping to ease her nerves a little and squeeze her hand.

"First we want you to know how terrible we feel about how we treated you when Brady was alive and more importantly when he passed away. We were so far out of line that it's embarrassing to us to see how we were to you. You did nothing but make our son happy and we didn't see it. That is until we found his letter to you." Mr. Carlyle says while holding onto his wife's hand on top of the table.

"Our son loved you and wanted to have a future with you but we tore that apart after he died. Now that you have been to the bank we pray that you'll start down the long road of forgiving us. We don't expect it now by any means but would like to know you're okay with what we've done for you over the years." Mrs. Carlyle says and reaches for Amie's hand but Amie pulls it back under the table.

"It's not something that will happen overnight. We would like to be a part of your life if at all possible. Someday. You are always welcome to come and visit us also." Mr. Carlyle finishes.

"Where is Brady buried?" Is all that Amie says to what they've both declared.

"Oh my goodness child you don't even know that do you? I am so ashamed of myself. I have to go. Please excuse me." Mrs. Carlyle stands up and heads for the double doors we came in.

"I'm sorry about that. Brady is buried in our family cemetery up on the hill of our estate. I will give the gatekeeper your name and grant you entrance anytime you want to go." He smiles at Amie and looks to me. "You'll take her?"

"Of course." I smile and squeeze Amie's hand again.

"So, I hear you like to play poker. I'm hosting a game tonight at the house if you're interested."

"Um, I don't play any longer. But thank you." How in the world did he find that out? Oh boy in his world it's probably easy to find out information on anyone. Amie looks at me so shocked she really doesn't know what to say either.

"We have plans tonight anyway, but thank you for the invite. And lunch." Amie spits out and stands to leave. I stand and shake Mr. Carlyle's hand but quickly follow Amie out. She is on fire and can't get out of here fast enough. I can't help but laugh because it's the complete opposite of what she was like when we came in.

Once we get to the cab I finally catch up to her and stop her before she can get inside. I turn her around and she looks so mad and her face is red.

"What's wrong Amie?"

"How dare he check into you like that! And to still offer you a spot at the table! I don't want to ever see that man or woman ever again!"

"Amie calm down. I really don't think he was trying to be nasty. He was trying to include me yes, but I don't think he meant anything by it."

"Can we go see Brady and then get out of this town?"

"Sure. Do you know where they live?"

"Yes." And she gives the address to the driver but the look on her face stays the same all the way there. She's really upset and I'm not sure what I'm supposed to say to calm her down either. Oh boy. I just sit back and wait for what's next.

26

Looking at this large cold stone with Brady's name on it leaves me feeling the loss all over again. I can't help but feel the tears start to roll down my cheeks but as they do I feel Aaron's arm go around me from the back and pull me to his front. How can I feel so lost and alone but also feel so happy and in love? In love? Whoa Amie this is the last place you need to be thinking about loving Aaron. You're at Brady's grave for God's sake get a grip!

"I'm ready to go." I pull away from Aaron and head for the waiting cab. I can't let Aaron's presence do this to me. I've worked too hard to get over the last failed relationship, I can't do another one. Especially since his family has been so wonderful to me. I would lose the jobs Amelia has lined up for me and my home, how could I forget that? I would be living out of my car again.

"Amie? Are you alright? You need to talk to me." Aaron finally breaks the silence in the cab.

Right before we pull up to the hotel he grabs my arm and turns me towards him. As soon as he does I see his body start to lean over to my side and his eyes are on my lips. The look on his face breaks my heart. This man is so wonderful how could I not have fallen in love with him? Yes, I have fallen 100% in love with Aaron. I just wish that thought didn't fill me with so much fear.

"I can't right now Aaron. Please just give me a few minutes alone before you come up. Today was very hard on me and I need to get my wits about me first." I kiss his cheek and exit the cab praying that he'll do as I asked. I race to the elevator and turn around inside to see him standing just inside the front doors to the hotel. He is doing just what I asked. Ah this man....

***

I don't know what's going on with Amie this time. I'm not sure I should have pushed her into lunch with the Carlyle's. But how was I to know it would turn into a visit to her ex-fiancé's grave? She's clearly in the middle of an inner battle right now and how can I blame her? She was thrust into one of the most painful times in her life by none other than me. I feel awful. She'll probably never forgive me for it either.

I decide to sit in the lobby and wait until Amie lets me know she's ready to talk. If that happens. It may be a long silent trip home if she doesn't.

I pull my phone out and call the only person I know that could help in this situation. Mom.

"Hi Ma. Yes, today was the meeting with the Carlyle's. It was good actually. Well, I thought it was. They apologized fully to Amie for everything they ever put her through. I think she was very overwhelmed though. Yes, and then she wanted to go to his grave so we went there. On their estate. Yes it was interesting. Now she hasn't spoken to me since. I don't know what to do Ma. I should never have pushed her into meeting with them. No I didn't say anything about the cemetery, that was all her. I don't really know what to think right now. She asked me to leave her alone for a while so I'm sitting in the lobby waiting. Well, calling you while I wait. Mom I really need your advice right now. You think

I should just leave her alone? Really? What do I do while I wait? Ok there's a coffee shop down the street I'll go wait there. Thanks Ma. Love you."

I hang up and start to walk towards the coffee shop but turn one last time in hopes that Amie has come off the elevator that just opened. No such luck. Just a young couple all over each other. You can clearly see the love that radiates off of them as they look at each other. Must be on their honeymoon. The mention of honeymoon makes me think of Amie in a bikini running in the ocean with me on our honeymoon. WHAT? Whoa Aaron that went quickly to another level. You can't love her. Women do nothing but take and leave. But Amie isn't like that. And she's the one with all the money now not me. I have nothing to offer her anyway, why would I even have a chance at marrying her?

Frustrated I walk out the hotel doors and head to the coffee shop. I must have a sour look on my face because no one smiles or greets me as I do. The barista asks what I would like and rushes to get my order ready; probably afraid I'll bite her head off. I'm a mess, how did this happen? I tried so hard not to fall in love with anyone but Amie snuck through my defenses. I sigh and turn around to find a little old man standing there watching me.

"Woman troubles?" He smiles and pats my arm not holding the hot coffee. I smile and nod my head. "Have a seat young man and I'll give you a piece of advice." So I sit and listen. I could use all the help I can get right now.

"Married or wanting to be?"

"Wanting I guess."

"Ah she snuck up on you did she? They have a way of doing that. Sneaky little buggars."

"You could say that yes. I tried so hard to keep her at arm's length but it didn't work."

"And now you're here alone and she's mad at you?"

I give him an astonished look and he smiles. "You're good at this. Why are you here and not with your lady?"

"I was with my lady for 52 years and when she passed away from cancer last year I had to figure out how to go on without her by my side. We wasted a lot of years trying not to love each other too but I'm so very thankful for the years we weren't fighting it."

"I haven't known Amie that long but she's such a wonderful person and I can't seem to get her out of my head. And now that she's mad at me I'm not sure what I'm supposed to do." I sigh and he pats me on the back.

"Son, if it's meant to be she'll come around. If her feelings are as strong as yours then she'll realize it too. Women have big hearts but overactive brains and sometimes those aren't in sync. They need time to figure out their own emotions before they can deal with ours. Let her have some space but make sure she knows you're here for her regardless."

"Is a text good enough?"

"In this day in age its fine. She'll then know you're still in this and give her the confidence in you that she is seeking."

"Thank you so much." I take out my cell phone and text Amie.

I'm here when you're ready to talk. However long it takes.

"Son, you are very welcome. Take care and let her know how you feel. Sooner rather than later." He slaps me on the back one more time and exits the coffee shop.

That one man's words helped to ease my mind and heart more than I think anyone has. I pray that Amie and I can be together for 52 or more years and still love each other that much, even after death.

27

A text from Aaron. What do I say back? My head says go talk to him but my heart says be careful. Which do I listen to?

How can I love someone so quickly and not know how to get him out of my head? This is insane. I haven't known him very long to feel like I can't live without him. I let out a big sigh and look at Aaron's text again. I start typing a reply before I realize it and hit send.

Gonna shower. Give me 30 mns and I'll be ready to talk.

During my long hot shower I ponder whether I'm upset about Brady or Aaron. Then it hits me that I'm upset with myself because I have let Aaron occupy so much of my thoughts and have pushed Brady out. I feel as if I'm cheating on Brady by loving Aaron. This is ridiculous. I can love them both. Right?

Just as I get out of the shower I hear my phone ringing and before I can answer I see it's Leah.

"Hi Leah. How are you feeling?"

"Good, how's the trip been? When are you coming home?"

"It's been great. I believe we're coming home tomorrow."

"You sound upset. Are you okay Amie? Has Aaron done something stupid again?"

"No. I'm just overwhelmed. We went to the bank, met with the Carlyle's and went to Brady's grave today."

"Oh wow all in one day?"

"Yes, all in one day. I'm so messed up inside. I feel like I'm cheating on Brady with my feelings for Aaron."

"Feelings? You love him don't you?"

"Yes, no matter how hard I tried not to, I fell in love with him. And now I feel guilty."

"I understand how you feel. When I met Austin I felt like I wasn't allowed to love anyone either or allowed to be happy again with what I went through with Lewis and losing Shannon. But Austin and his family helped me to heal and understand that I'm allowed to love again. And it's been the greatest love of my life."

"On one hand I feel that way but there's something that tells me I can't love Aaron this soon either."

"You need to follow your heart Amie. Your heart will show you what it needs. There's no rush so take the time you need to figure it all out. Aaron will wait, I promise."

"Thank you Leah I can't begin to tell you how much I appreciate your help. I think you've helped me decide where my heart is telling me to go."

"I pray it's in Aaron's direction. But no pushing! Talk to you tomorrow when you get home. Come by when you're back so we can chit chat."

"Bye, thanks again." I hang up feeling lighter and happier than I have in years. I also feel excited and nervous to talk to Aaron. I have to tell him how I feel and pray he feels the same.

***

I stand outside of our hotel room feeling like a scared little school boy. I don't think I've been this nervous since my first kiss in 7th grade. If I tell Amie that I love her and she laughs back in my face I'm going to want to crawl in a hole and never come out.

I finally get the courage to knock on the door and wait with my heart in my throat. Just as I'm afraid she's changed her mind, the door opens and the most beautiful woman I have ever seen is standing just inside the room. I feel like my heart has stopped and I'm in Heaven. She smiles and my heart skips a beat reassuring me that I'm not dead yet.

"Aaron? Are you okay?" I hear her soft, caring voice ask. I try to speak but the words just won't come out so I nod like a dumb little boy. "Are you sure? Say something."

"I'm fine. You look so beautiful and I'm at a loss for words."

"For once you have nothing to say?" She says with a big grin on her face. Her eyes light up when she laughs and I hope to see and hear her laugh for the rest of my life.

"Yes." I say as she motions me inside the room. The world seems to be spinning as I follow her in and shut the door behind me. We're alone and I know I need to get to talking before the moment is over but I can't get the words to come out.

"Let me start. Okay?" I nod once again. Dumb little boy. She turns me into a dumb little boy every time. I smile at the thought of our little boy and what he would look like.

"Not sure I wanna know what you're smiling about."

"Probably not. Go ahead." I sit down in a chair next to the bed while she sits on the bed itself. I can tell she's struggling to find the words too so I reach over and take her hand. I rub the back of it with my thumb hoping to comfort her enough to help get the words out.

"Aaron when I came to Colvin, I never intended to find people that would embed themselves so far into my life and heart that I can't imagine being without them. Your mother started that with the first job she hired me for. The rest of your family have been there alongside her to make me feel welcome and included in anything going on. Yes, it helped living in the garage apartment but everything else they've helped with has meant the world to me. And then there came the long lost oldest son that moved home in a whirlwind and seemed to stick with me like a magnet. You inserted yourself into my life and heart so far that I don't think I could ever live without you Aaron. It scared me to death to feel the things I was for you when I should have been grieving Brady but I did that grieving years ago and I'm ready to move on and be happy again. With you. I love you so much Aaron." She finishes with tears running down her face and my heart just breaks and jumps for joy at the same time.

I kneel down in front of her and pull her into my arms. "Amie I love you more than I have ever loved anyone. I never knew I was able to love anyone this much. Or wanted to. You stormed the walls around my heart and now I pray you'll never leave. I want to have a family with you and love you for the rest of my life. You make me whole and now I realize you were the missing piece I've always been searching for. Will you marry me Amie?"

"YES! YES! YES!" We stand up and embrace as if we'd been apart for days. This woman makes my heart so happy and I can't wait for her to be my wife.

"I'll get you a ring as soon as I can, I promise."

"I don't care about that. I only care about marrying you and living forever as your wife and partner."
"Partner?"

"In your construction company. I want to give you the funds you need to get going and then we'll be set."

"I don't know about that. I don't want to owe my wife tons of money."

"It's our money Aaron. It's not mine."

"Until we're married it's yours."

"Then let's get married right now. I'm sure we could find someone to do it before the night is out."

"Seriously? You're up for that? You don't want the big huge wedding?"

"Oh no. I've planned too many of those over the years and I'm over that hoopla."

"So we're doing this right now? We're going to have a very upset family back in Colvin if they aren't included."

"True. Let's call them and see if they can come. You call your mom, she'll handle it and they'll all be here."

28

Today everyone will arrive from Colvin for the wedding. I let Aaron call everyone and make the arrangements but I am meeting Leah, Karlie and Amelia at a bridal boutique this morning to get a dress. When I think of trying on wedding dresses it makes the butterflies start in my stomach. I haven't thought about getting married since before Brady passed away and never thought it was in the cards for me since. I wish my mother could be here to enjoy these pre-wedding moments with me. We used to talk about my wedding when I was little but neither of us ever dreamed she wouldn't be around for it.

Getting overwhelmed with emotion I sigh deeply and shake my head to clear my mind a little. Today is supposed to be happy not sad. Just as I start to recover I hear Aaron come out of the bathroom. I look at him and see my future and realize there's no reason to worry about the past and what I don't have. We are getting married and his family is amazing so there's nothing to be sad about. Yes I wish my own family was here but I know they'll be watching from Heaven, they wouldn't miss it.

"What? Something wrong?" He says when he sees me staring at him.

"No. It's perfect actually." I walk up to him and wrap my arms around his neck and kiss him like I've never kissed him before.

"Wow what was that for?" He says breathlessly when I let go.

"Nothing. Just showing you how much I love you and how excited I am to marry you tomorrow."

"I love you too. When are you meeting the girls?"

"In an hour. I better go get ready. You're meeting the guys in an hour too? Have they arrived yet?"

"Yep, plane just landed. I'm gonna make a few calls and head out while you're getting ready. I love you." He kisses me goodbye and I step into the bathroom to ready myself for the wedding whirlwind that's about to begin. I pause and smile knowing how exciting it's going to be marrying the man that healed my heart. I say a quick thank you to Brady and my parents for sending me to Colvin. Without their help I might not be this happy right now.

***

"Did you bring it?" I ask Dad when he answers the phone. I'm walking down the hallway after leaving our hotel room.

"Yes Son, I have it. The people in the airport looked at me funny carrying this big thing but I got it."

"She's going to love it. Thank you. Can I talk to Ma right quick?"

"Hi Aaron. How are you feeling? How's Amie?"

"We're great Ma. Do you think she'll be okay with us getting that photo of her parents and blowing it up and framing it like that? It won't upset her will it?"

"No Aaron I believe she'll absolutely love it. It will show her that we deeply care about her and want her parents to be a part of the ceremony even when they're not here to do it in person. It was very thoughtful."

"Are you guys through baggage claim yet?"

"Yes. We're headed to get taxis now. We'll take two, one for the guys and one for the girls."

"Great. Tell Dad and the guys I'll see them at the tux shop in a few. Love you all. Thanks for coming on such short notice."

"We wouldn't miss it for the world Aaron. We love you. See ya soon."

I have the best family ever. I can't believe I spent so much time running away from them and Colvin. So much time wasted that could have been spent making memories with them instead of without me. I will never let that happen again, that's for sure. Amie and I will be the best Aunt and Uncle to our nieces and nephews. And parents to ours. That makes my heart skip a beat and a big smile come across my face. I can't wait to see Amie with a baby growing inside her or the little ones running around that look just like her and I. That's going to be so amazing to see. I picked the most amazing woman to have children with too. This time I know she wants them also. The difference between my first marriage and this one is like night and day.

***

"Hi!!! I can't believe we're doing this! It's so exciting!" Karlie yells and runs to hug me once their taxi arrives in front of the bridal shop. I hug her back and can't help but feel a huge smile spread across my face too.

"I know what you mean! It's surreal!" I hug Leah and Amelia too.

"Someone else wants you to hug her." Karlie points to Aleah. She's squirming for me to pick her up out of the stroller.

I lean down to pick her up and she smiles the biggest most amazing kid smile I've ever seen. It hits me that Aaron and I could start on a family of our own too! How exciting to have a couple kids running around that look like Aaron and myself.

"Hi there sweet girl. I couldn't forget about you! How did you like your plane ride today?" I kiss Aleah's forehead and squeeze her tight.

"Let's get inside and get started, we have a million things to get done today if we're pulling off a wedding tomorrow." Amelia says and ushers us girls inside the boutique; all of us with big smiles on our faces.

"Welcome. You must be the Benjamin/Blake family?"

"Yes ma'am. I'm Amie Benjamin."

"The bride!" Leah exclaims.

"Yes, I'm the bride. That's so weird to say though. I'm getting married!!!"

"Follow me and we'll get started on finding that dress." We all follow the sales lady into a room full of rows and rows of wedding dresses. I hear everyone gasp in shock at the amount of them.

"I know it looks overwhelming but if you'll just tell me which style and color you're looking for we can narrow it down quickly."

"I'm not sure actually."

"Ok, we'll start with a few different styles and then see which you like the best then we can narrow down to that one style after you choose it." She takes off leaving us standing there still in shock looking at each other.

"Wow. We have only a few hours to do this?" I hear Audrey say sarcastically making everyone else laugh.

"We'll get it done in time, I promise." We startle to see the sales lady back again with an arm full of dresses. "Right this way to the dressing room. The rest of you ladies can have a seat in the other room in front of the mirrors. If there aren't enough chairs, let me know and we'll get more." I smile and follow her leaving the rest of my comfort zone behind.

***

"Son, I'm thinking this tux is a little bit much don't you?"

"Dad, this is a very important day to Amie and me. I want her to know I'm all in so we have to dress the part. It's only for a few hours."

"Ok, I guess I'll comply then. Just know I'm hating it the whole time. Good thing I care about the girl!" He slaps me on the back and walks back to the mirror. I smile and keep adjusting my bowtie.

"You all look great." I say and look at my brothers and brother in law. I never dreamed I'd be looking at them getting fitted for my wedding. I missed the fittings for their weddings but look at them rushing to be here for mine. I feel a pang of guilt come across me and I say. "I can't begin to tell you how much it means to me that you guys flew here at a moment's notice. I know I haven't been a very good brother and son in the past but you guys are amazing. I love you. Thank you."

"We wouldn't dream of missing it. We know you were busy Aaron. We knew when you found what you were looking for you'd come home. Everything happens for a reason. We always knew you loved us, which we never doubted." Dad says and hugs me once more with the others following suit.

"I think that's enough sappy stuff. Since we've all found our penguin suits, let's pay and get outta here. Let's meet the girls for lunch and get the rest of our list done." We pay and get out of the store just in time for a white limo to pull up in front of the tux shop as we walk outside.

We see a window in the back roll down and a red head pop out. "Handsome men need a ride?" Karlie yells and smiles.

"Where did you ladies find this chariot?" Dad asks as he climbs in ahead of the rest of us guys.

"Leah rented it for us. It's all ours as long as we need it." Ma smiles and kisses Dad as he sits next to her in the front of the limo.

"Wow babe you hit it out of the park." Austin sits next to Leah and kisses her while patting her belly.

"Hi there handsome." I hear a familiar voice say as I climb in last. My heart jumps as I look into the most beautiful woman's eyes I've ever seen.

"Beautiful, how are you? Get your dress?" I kiss her full lips and feel her sigh.

"I did. It's beautiful I can't wait for you to see it."

"I can't wait to see you in it either. I love you." I kiss her again and we head off to find a restaurant for lunch.

***

"We want to thank you all for coming on such short notice. We love you all so much and wouldn't want to get married without you being here." I loop my arm in Aaron's because I'm starting to get overcome with emotion as we stand in front of his family at dinner. He sees that I'm getting emotional so he takes over the speech.

"You guys are the best family and friends we could ask for and we're blessed to share this special event with you. We wouldn't want to do this without you. We may not have known each other very long but we both know without a doubt that we've found our soul mate. We love you and pray you know how much. Once again, thanks for coming all this way on short notice to enjoy the day with us. Cheers." We all clink glasses together and begin to eat. I am so blessed to be starting a new life with this family. None of us could be happier and or more excited for the wedding.

***

After we get back to the hotel Aaron and I stop just outside my hotel room. He's staying with his parents tonight so that he doesn't see me before the wedding. Bad luck is something we do not need tomorrow.

"Well, babe I'm going to let you get your beauty rest for tomorrow. I have a few last minute things I want to get done before I go to bed. I love you and look forward to marrying you. I'll see you when you walk down that aisle towards me. Sweet dreams." He kisses me on the forehead and lips before squeezing my hand and ushering me inside my hotel room.

"I love you Aaron. I can't wait to be your wife. Sleep well my love."

"Are you excited?" I hear from Audrey once I shut the door and turn back around to face the crowd of smiling women in my room.

"Wow, I didn't know you were all in here. What's going on?"

"We're going to have a mini bachelorette party in the room!" Leah exclaims and puts a sash over my head that says BRIDE.

"Oh my goodness you ladies are amazing! Thank you." I start to tear up at their thoughtfulness.

"No crying missy. This is a very happy occasion so nothing but happy thoughts." Amelia says and hugs me.

"No more crying not even happy tears. What else do you ladies have planned?" I wipe away the tears and decide it's time to stop with the boo hoo-ing and be happy.

29

I marry the most amazing woman I've ever met today. I'm the one that gets to give her my last name and spend the rest of my life with. She and I will raise children together and I can't wait. The anxiety level is high but it's a good kind. I'm anxious to say "I do" and hear Amie say the same back. As I attach the last button on my jacket I hear someone enter the room.

"Oh Aaron you look so handsome. Amie's going to swoon when she sees you in your tux. I'm so proud of you and the man you've become." I wrap my arms around her and pull her close. The love this woman has for us kids and just about anyone she comes across is amazing. She has the biggest heart and takes anyone in that needs a helping hand. I'm so glad she came across Amie or I might not be marrying her right now.

"Love you Ma. I'm so sorry I didn't come home for so long."

"That's all in the past now. No going back. We all look to the future and the happiness that awaits you and Amie. I better go now before my makeup starts to run. Leah's guy worked so hard on our hair and makeup I would hate to ruin it. See you later son."

"See you in the there. You look beautiful Ma."

"Are you monopolizing my wife?" We hear Dad say from the doorway. "But you're exactly right, she looks outstanding."

"Well thank you two but I really do need to go do one last check on the girls before the ceremony starts." She pats me on the shoulder and walks out the door shutting it behind her.

"You ready for this?"

"Yes sir. More than ready."

"I am proud of you Aaron. You've overcome the worst and now look at you. You're marrying an amazing woman today."

"Thanks Dad. Could you take this letter to Amie for me?"

"Of course. I'll see you out there in a few." He also pats me on the shoulder before leaving the room.

***

Today's the day I'm marrying Aaron. He's the perfect package and I can't imagine my life without him now. Especially now that I have fallen in love with his wonderful family too.

"Hi sweet girl can I come in?" Amelia says as she cracks the door to my room. I look over at her and smile.

"Of course you can. Please come in." I reach for her and lean in to place a small kiss on her cheek.

"You look absolutely gorgeous Amie. Aaron is going to stop breathing as soon as he sees you walking down that aisle."

"Ah thank you. I feel good too. How's he doing? Have you seen him yet?"

"Just left his room and he's very anxious to marry the woman of his dreams." She smiles and squeezes my forearm.

"I love him so much Amelia. I just wish my parents could be here today but I know they're here in spirit."

"Don't let the emotions spill out. We've been in hair and makeup way too long to endure it again!" She laughs.

"True. I'm ready to get this started. I want to marry my soul mate and start our life together."

"Well, I'm going to go let everyone know we're ready to start. Take your time and come out when you're ready. You do look beautiful Amie. I'm so proud to welcome you to our family as my daughter. We love you too not just Aaron." She hugs me one more time before slipping back out the door.

I sigh deep and let the air out slowly. My emotions are all over the place. The butterflies in my stomach are in overdrive.

   knock knock

I walk to the door and pray it's not Aaron saying he's changed his mind. "Aaron? Is that you?"

"It's AJ. Can I come in for a second?"

"Oh please do. Come on in. You look very handsome AJ!"

"Thank you and can I say that you look stunning Amie. Your parents would be so happy and proud of you if they were here."

He hugs me tight and hands me a small envelope.

"Aaron asked me to deliver this to you before the ceremony started." I take the envelope from him and feel a bit woozy not sure what's inside. The last time I had an envelope to open my whole world changed.

"What is it?"

"I honestly don't know he just gave it to me and asked me to deliver it to you. I will go so you can open it in private."

"No, please stay. I wanted to ask if you would be interested in walking me down the aisle today. I know I'm not your daughter but without my own father here I would very much like you to do the honors."

"Oh Amie I would be the so honored to walk you down the aisle to my son. Thank you for asking." He wraps me up once more.

As soon as I get free of those big arms I start to open the envelope.

My lovely wife-to-be,

First off I want to say I am so very excited to be marrying you today. You're the most amazing person I've ever met and I'm very proud to be able to call you my wife.

I know you're missing your parents today most of all but please know that they are here and are very happy and proud of you for what you've overcome. They above all know how wonderful you are and that you deserve the world.

I plan on spending the rest of my life trying to live up to what they would expect of the man you marry. Please know that they will be here walking with you as you come towards me and join me in life.

I love you more than these words could ever express and I can't wait to spend the rest of my life making you happy. See you at the ceremony and then we will forever be one.

All my love forever,
Aaron

Oh my goodness how am I supposed to stay dry eyed after that?
AJ must have seen me struggling to keep them at bay and hands
me a tissue.
"Wipe those tears and let's go join the rest of our family."

I do just that and take AJ's arm while heading off to start the rest
of this wonderful life Aaron and I are going to have.

30

Dad's walking her down the aisle. That has to be the most amazing thing he could have done for Amie. My heart melts a little more when I see the way he's looking down at her as if she were his flesh and blood.

I then look over at the two chairs that we had set out for her parents. Just where they were supposed to be if they were here. Instead there's a picture of each one taking their place. Then waiting in our honeymoon suite there's the large picture my parents had blown up and framed for Amie to ensure her parents always have a place in our home. She's going to love it; at least I hope she does.

I see her gaze lock with mine after a few long seconds. She is breathtaking and I'm at a total loss of words, not even sure if I'm still breathing. I do know I've got a few rogue tears finding their way out.

I'm broken out of my fog by Austin tugging on my arm so I look over at him and he's standing there with a huge grin.

"She's beautiful, brother." I smile and nod not sure I could form anything else. As I'm turning my head back towards my bride I catch a glimpse of Dad looking at Mom with the most content and happy look on his face. They love Amie about as much as I do which makes my heart feel even fuller. I'm not just gaining a wife but they're gaining another daughter and my siblings are gaining another sister. We're giving Amie what she's wanted since her parents passed away. A family to love her unconditionally.

***

Walking towards Aaron on the arm of his father I feel so loved and protected. This feeling is something I wasn't sure I would ever find for myself. Once my parents were gone I was alone until Brady, then he was also gone. I lift my eyes again and see Aaron's smiling face and see the tears running down his handsome face. That makes my heart jump as I finally realize just how much this man loves me. Possibly as much as I love him. And his family. Oh my goodness this family is so amazing too. His brothers are standing up next to him while his sister and sisters in law are standing on my side for me. And who could forget the strong man walking me down the aisle.

I look up at AJ and smile as we near the end by Aaron. I feel another hand touch my shoulder and I turn to see the angel herself, Amelia. I owe so much to this woman. I hug her tightly and then AJ before they hand me off to Aaron. I smile the biggest and most heartfelt smile I could muster as he takes my hand and we walk to our spot in front of the Reverend. If I'm not mistake this is the same one that's married each of the Blake children. These people really are a force to be reckoned with. I can't keep the tears from slipping out now but Aaron stops them with his thumbs and smiles a heart stopping smile. It took nothing but that moment to calm my emotions and settle myself down. This is what I'm supposed to be doing and everything is just how it's meant to be.

The Reverend asks if we could all take a small moment of silence for my parents and motions towards two chairs that I now see have pictures of my parents on them. Tears are coming now regardless. Who did this? Oh my that's so amazing that they included my parents today.

Aaron turns me back towards him and says, "Mom and Dad knew you would want them here."

I look at Amelia and AJ and mouth the words "thank you". They nod and smile. I look over once again at Mom and Dad then at the man I plan to spend the rest of my life with.

***

"Aaron you may kiss your bride." You don't have to tell me twice. I put a hand on each side of Amie's beautiful face and kiss her lips as if I were a dying man. I can't imagine loving this woman any more than I do now. My heart is literally overflowing with emotion as I kiss my wife. My wife. I smile as we hear hoot and hollers coming from the audience and Amie smiles up at me I can clearly see that she feels the exact same way I do.

"I am proud to introduce Mr. & Mrs. Aaron Blake." We start down the aisle and get hit with something that feels like the rice you hear about people throwing after weddings. I look down and realize its just confetti in the shape of wedding bells. Someone thought of everything.

"Are you ready to go to the reception? They're holding the back room at the restaurant for us." I ask my new wife and kiss her lips once more.

"Yes. I'm starving and need a drink. My emotions are all over the place." She says as she slips her arms around my waist and lays her head on my chest. I can't help but wrap my arms around her and pull her as tight against me as possible. This really just happened. I just married this incredible person and it feels so right. The last time I did this I felt so unsettled. Probably because these people weren't there with us. No, I wasn't with Amie that's why it wasn't right.

"I love you Mrs. Blake." I look down at her and her up at me.

She smiles and says, "I love you Mr. Blake." I lean down and kiss her sweet lips again but when it lingers a little too long I hear Aiden say something to break us out of our special moment.

"Okay, okay let's go eat. I have the rest of my life to make out with my wife." I can hear Amie giggle and start to follow the others into the restaurant.

"Congratulations Mr. & Mrs. Blake." We hear all the staff and customers say as we pass through the room towards the back private room.

"I can't imagine a more perfect wedding and reception. You all did such an amazing job pulling it together. We couldn't have done it without you." Amie says and hugs each and every one of our family members present. Our family. That sounds so amazing.

"Cheers to the newlyweds! You two deserve the very best and we all know you'll have exactly that. We love you." Dad says and everyone clinks the glasses of champagne we were handed by the wait staff.

"And we love you." I say and kiss my bride one more time.

"I have one more surprise for you Amie. Dad can you bring it in?" Dad walks to the next room and brings back a large blob of fabric.

"Aaron. What have you done now?"

"I wanted you to always know that your parents are here no matter what we're doing or where we are. There a part of you and for that I'm so very thankful. So, Mom and Dad helped me get this photo blown up and framed for our house. Our house. Wherever that might be. Even the small apartment above the garage at the 6AB."

I uncover the picture and hear everyone gasp and Amie's tears start to flow. I think she's been holding onto them all day but can't any longer. I wrap my arms around her from behind as she looks at the picture. She keeps mumbling sweet words for me but no one can understand because she's crying so hard. I can tell they're for me because she's also squeezing my hands tight.

"Aaron I love you." That's all she can get out as she turns and buries herself in my arms. I smile at everyone as they take their seats to await dinner.

31

Six months later.....

"Aaron what are you doing up there? We don't have time for your childish antics." I hear Monica say to Aaron as he's coming down the ladder. She and I have become quite the female team against him.

"If you must know I was making sure the gutter was attached properly. What did you think I was doing? Taking a nap on the roof?" He frowns and grabs my hand. "Are you two going to gang up on me during every project?"

"I moved here to help you didn't I?" Monica says and puts her hands on her hips. She's ready to battle it out so I think I'll slip away and get some more of my own work done. We've been planning a baby shower for Leah and Austin since we got back from the honeymoon.

"Where are you going my love?" He caught me just as I was about to slip away.

"Work. I do have my own company to run. Double B Construction is your baby. Parties by Benjie is mine."

"Okay I guess I'll let you go but I'll be by later to see how you're doing."

"Aaron, you haven't let me out of your sight since we got home from the honeymoon. I'll be okay on my own for a few hours."

"No, I promised to never let you be alone again remember?"

"This is a little extreme big man. I'll see you later. I love you." I kiss his pouty lips and leave the job site. Goodness that man's going to smother me.

"Karlie, I'm headed to the office if you wanna stop by. Your brother in law is driving me crazy. He won't let me out of his sight like I'm going to crumble."

"He loves you and knows how hard your life was before you came here."

"I know but goodness. I'm capable of spending time alone without wanting to cry for goodness sakes."

"Ok, well I'll head to the office in a few. Aleah's a little fussy right now but I'll let Amelia watch her for a bit. That should make them both happy."

I hang up and place the cell phone in the car's cup holder. I look to the left again and see Aaron standing in the doorway of the house he's building waving goodbye to me. My heart constricts and I realize that no matter how smothering he gets, he is just doing it because he wants me to be happy. I wave and blow him a kiss.

***

"You're going to smother the poor girl Aaron. Lighten up dude."

"Shut up Monica. I brought you here to help run the business side of Double B not how to treat my wife." I scowl at her and walk away to find the crew.

"I'm telling you she's a big girl that doesn't need your attention 24/7. Lighten up Aaron."

"I said shut up. Go do some paperwork or something." I slam the back door before she can say anything else to me.

I know she's right but I can't help but want to spend every waking moment with Amie. I love having a wife and having her close to me. I guess I'd probably get a lot more work done if I let go of her though. I smile thinking I've turned into a crazy touchy feely person since I married Amie. Good grief, man up! Haha.

"Hey guys where's that new guy from Tulsa?" I look around for the friend of Maysen's that I just hired yesterday. It was a favor to my brother in law but I'm not so sure it was a smart choice.

"I think he's over there on the other side of the garage talking to Monica." I start towards that spot as I hear her speaking loudly and not very nicely.

"Hey, hey what's going on here? Monica are you okay?" I step in between Monica and the new guy.

"I'm okay. This loser thought he could hit on me and it would actually work." She crosses her arms making herself look even grumpier.

"Why aren't you working? I'm paying you to work. As a favor to Maysen. Get over there and do just that." I motion to the rest of the crew and he walks away hanging his head. "You just denied him in front of everyone. That's cruel, even for you. Maybe you were around the she-devil too long." I smile and step back awaiting her attempt at hitting me.

"You're terrible. Go follow your wife around like a puppy dog a little more and leave me alone!" She exclaims. I think I hit a nerve. I snicker as she storms off. Score one for Aaron.

***

"So how was your day my love?" I ask Aaron as he comes in the door of the apartment. I've been home about an hour and about have supper finished.

Aaron walks over to me and wraps me up in his arms. I sigh at the feeling of being in my favorite spot.

"I'm sorry I'm smothering you. Monica set me straight. I won't anymore I promise. I just love spending every waking moment with you."

"I know babe, I love you and love spending time with you too but I do need a few minutes to spend getting my own work done. Will you set the table?"

"Sure. No one's joining us tonight? That's shocking."

"Nope. I told everyone we needed a night alone to talk so they're off doing their own things in their own houses."

"Ma too? I bet she took that well." He smiles and starts to set the table just as I asked.

"She was fine once I told her we wanted some alone time. I'm sure you know what she's hoping for."

"Babies. My family thinks that's the only outcome from alone time I guess."

"I guess."
"Not that I would mind a little Amie though." He slips his hands up under my shirt from behind me while I'm standing at the stove stirring the sauce for spaghetti.

"Aaron James Blake, get the table set so we can eat before this burns."

"Yes ma'am."

"You're terrible. You and your family have a one track mind."

"I know I know. I can't help but want to touch you. And you did say you'd love me for better or worse."

"Not to have sex at any time of the day!" I laugh and step back from his advance once more.

"It was implied." He catches me when I back up against the counter.

"Are you sure we don't have time before this is all done?"

"Aaron!"

"Okay, okay we'll eat first."

"Terrible!" I laugh and shake my head. He's like an ornery teenager that can't keep his hands to himself. Not that I mind, just love to tease my husband.

"So, how's the new guy doing that's friends with Maysen? Audrey's really worried he'll be too much of a handful."

"Well, he hit on Monica today and she set him straight. He's not a bad worker if he'd actually work. He's definitely a ladies man."

"Poor Monica. I can't imagine what it's like having an overzealous man around all day." I smile and wait for Aaron to get my joke.

"Funny. I could sleep on the couch for a while if you'd like."

"Ha ha not a chance." I try to ignore the look he's giving me knowing he got the best of me instead. "Just eat."

"Yes ma'am. Need my strength."

"Terrible!" I smile and throw a slice of French bread at him.

32

"Hello there, I'm looking for Aaron Blake." Amelia hears as she opens her front door and sees a strange woman standing in front of her. This woman looks as if she came straight off the catwalk in London.

"I'm sorry but who are you?"

"Who are you? The housekeeper?"

"Well, I guess you could say that yes but I am also his mother. I'm going to ask one for time ma'am who you are. And if you don't answer I'll call the hands and have you removed from the property!"

"Well, it's so nice to finally meet you. I'm Aaron's wife." She holds out her hand to shake Amelia's but Amelia just stares at her, rather glares at her. She's heard the horror stories about this woman there's no way she'll play nice with her.

"You must be Payton."

"Yes ma'am. Where did you say my husband was?"

"Your ex-husband is probably at work. I'm not so sure you're going to be a welcome sight."

"Oh he'll be excited to see me don't you worry."

"His new construction site is over by the high school in town. You can't miss it. Don't say I didn't warn you though." And Amelia shuts the front door before the evil witch could say another word.

She runs to the kitchen to get her cell phone to make a warning call that will definitely be welcome.

"Hi Amie just wanted to call and let you know that Aaron's ex-wife was just here looking for him. Yes, I told her she wasn't going to get a very happy welcome but she's very determined, I guess you could say. Yes, she just went out the 6AB gates. No, I thought maybe you could go rescue my son. Thanks Amie. Good luck and can't wait to hear how this battle goes."

***

"Well if that isn't a sight for sore eyes. I always did love seeing you stretched out on a ladder." I freeze as I hear that wretched voice. I could recognize it anywhere. But here? What the heck is that woman doing here?

Without turning around I say, "What are you doing here? You're a long way from the big city."

"Oh Aaron how I have missed your snide remarks."

"I have to say I haven't missed a thing about you. Once again, what are you doing here? And how in the world did you find me?"

"My mother in law told me where I could find you."

"She's not your mother in law. Last I heard you were married to a cheat."

"She's a wonderful woman by the way. I see why you hated coming home."

"Very funny. I'm not going to ask you again, what are you doing here Payton?"

"I came to see you. I've missed you."

"I highly doubt that. Seriously what are you doing here?" I'm getting irritated.

"I've been hearing rumors swirling around that you were starting a new company and pulling a lot of the crew members and vendors we use."

"Well, now you see it's true so you can go."

"No, I want to see what's going on here. You really have started from the ground up again haven't you? Kinda like a Phoenix rising from the ashes. When's the last time you bet your entire life on a game of cards?"

"You know exactly when that was. I haven't touched a playing card since."

"I find that hard to believe. You lived to play in those games. That's why it was so easy to get you to Vegas."

"Well believe it. It took me losing it all to find where I belong and what I want to do."

"You loved AB though."

"Yes I did but I've since figured out that I didn't like all of it. It got too commercialized and too centered around money. Here I get to help people and make a difference."

"You sound like a public service commercial. Gag me."

"It's true. You have AB what else do you want?"

"I want you to come back with me Aaron."

"What?! Why in the hell would I do that?"

"Because you can have AB back and be back in the center of life again. We could be good together again."

"Not a chance lady." We both hear from the opposite end of the garage where I had been fixing the door opener.

"And who the heck do you think you are coming in here talking to me like that. You must be the cleaning lady here or something. Run along and clean something like he pays you to do."

"Run along cleaning lady? You must be Payton."

"Yes and who might you be? And why are you still standing here? I said go do something you're paid to do. You should fire this one Aaron she's very unruly."

I can't help but smile at the sight of my ex-wife trying to dismiss my new wife and business partner without having a clue who she is.

"Nah I think I'll keep her." I reach for Amie and wrap her up in my arms and plant a big long kiss on her lips. I can hear the giant gasp come from Payton as I do.

"What in the world are you doing Aaron? Degraded yourself to sleeping with the workers now? What has happened to you?"

"I am sleeping with this woman yes. She's my wife. Amie as you can tell this is Payton, Payton this is my wife Amie."

"Wife?!? I can't believe it. You married someone else so soon? You just moved down here not that long ago."

"So? When you find the one you can't let them get away. You were clearly not the one. Still not and never will be. I think it's time for you to go. There's nothing here for you and I without a doubt will not be going back to the city with you."

"Why are you staying here in this horrid little town? Everyone was smiling and waving on my way over here. It was so creepy."

"I actually love it here. I always have but I got too caught up in the hustle and bustle to remember that until Amie reminded me."

"Well Suzy Homemaker will do just fine tending to the cows and chickens while you come back to the real world Aaron. This isn't you."

"You wouldn't know me from the door man. Don't pretend to know me. What does your husband have to say about you coming out here?"

"We aren't together anymore. He wouldn't care less where I am."

"Well for that I'm sorry but you're not wanted here either. I am beyond happy here in Colvin and never intend to leave. I'm sorry you're lost right now but you have to do it somewhere else."

"And with someone other than my husband. You had your chance, you blew it." Amie says and crosses her arms across her chest. She's so beautiful when she's mad.

"Wow. You never looked at me like that Aaron. You do love her." Tears start to well up in Payton's eyes before she turns to go.

"Good bye Payton. Take care and try to find happiness."

"If you ever change your mind I'll be waiting." And she gets in her car and drives away.

"What just happened here?" I turn around and ask Amie who seems to be calm as a cucumber about this. I would think she'd be so shocked she would be fuming.

"That would be the Wicked Witch of the North. She flew in on her broomstick this morning looking to kidnap you." She wraps her arms around my waist and leans her head against my chest.

"You're awfully calm about this. My mother must have called you when she left the Ranch."

"Yes she did. She sent me to rescue you." She smiles up at me and melts my insides like she always does.

"I love you Mrs. Blake."

"The last Mrs. Blake."

"Definitely."

"I love you Mr. Blake."

"We better go fill Ma in on the outcome. She's probably pacing inside the front door." I smile and put my hand on the small of Amie's back and walk to the pickup with her. I can seriously picture my mother pacing the floor wondering what's going on over here. Kinda surprising she sent Amie instead of coming herself.

33

"It was hilarious seeing the look on her face when she realized that I was his wife not the cleaning lady." I say as we retell the story to Amelia and the whole family at dinner.

"I can't believe she had the guts to come out here and try to get you to go back with her." AJ says trying to follow the conversation going on with every family member chiming in.

"She's desperate and alone. She thinks I'm the only man who can help her but little does she know she's the scariest woman most of the crew has ever met. She would do just fine on her own if she just let go of being so mean and spoiled."

"She isn't a nice person that's for sure Aaron. I'm really not sure what you saw in her." I smirk at my husband and try to hide the fact that I really don't see what he was doing with someone like that.

"That goes to show you the type of person he was before he came home." Amelia says with a calm and loving voice. She knows that Aaron was a mess before and when he came back to Colvin. She would have done anything to not let him go through what he did.

"I was a different person that's for sure. I honestly don't recognize the person I was. After seeing her today I completely understand why I needed to hit rock bottom. I'm glad I did so that I could make my way back here. And especially to Amie."

"Ah the big brother is a little softy now. Who would've thunk it? Wait until you have kids." Aiden says and winks at Karlie.

"Speaking of kids, has anyone heard from Leah and Austin? She had a checkup earlier this afternoon but we haven't heard how it went." Amelia asks hoping someone has information.

"No need to wonder anymore. They just pulled up." AJ points out the window to where they did just pull up. We see Austin go around and help a very pregnant Leah out of the passenger side. She looks miserable. We're all beginning to think that baby never wants to come out.

"That poor girl looks miserable." I say as everyone gets up to go help them in the door.

"There you are! Mom was just asking if anyone had heard from you this afternoon." Aiden says to Austin and Leah. Austin pulls out the chair for Leah but she shakes her head no.

"You don't wanna stay for dinner?" Amelia asks as she sees the gesture.

"It's not that. I'm afraid to leak on your chairs. We're in labor and they're waiting for my water to break. They induced me this afternoon." She smiles and awaits the cheers.

"Oh my goodness Leah we're so excited for you two!" Audrey says and hugs Leah and Austin before anyone else can get there.

"So it's truly happening anytime?"

"The doc says Leah and the baby aren't exactly on the same page yet but they're getting close. Her body isn't ready but the baby seems to be. So, they told us to go home and relax then if her water does break to come back because it should progress pretty quickly after that."

"What happens if her water doesn't break?" I ask not really knowing since I've never had kids of my own. Everyone else seems to nod in agreement with that question.

"They said if she hadn't progressed enough to have the baby in the morning they would probably schedule a C-section for tomorrow afternoon."

"So you'll be parents most likely by the end of day tomorrow?" Audrey squeals and hugs them again. Maysen finally pulls her back to where he's standing to allow Leah and Austin to get hugs from the rest of us.

"Did they say how you could help it along a little?" Amelia says and everyone laughs because she is clearly beyond excited to meet her new grandchild.

"Actually they said walking would help the most. So, after we eat maybe we can all go for a walk?" Leah says and sits this time in the chair Austin was holding out for her.

"Don't worry about the chair sweetheart I can always get a new one." Amelia smiles and motions for the rest of us to sit also.

"Now back to the task at hand. Who would like some dinner?" AJ laughs and gets a large scoop of mashed potatoes.

We look around at the other men and they're doing the same thing. Food is their #1 priority isn't it? We all laugh when they freeze and realize we're watching them dig in like a pack of wild dogs.

34

The next morning Amie and I are sitting in the kitchen eating breakfast when my phone chimes with a message.

Still no baby. C-section at 3.

I read the text and look up at Amie. She's leaning clear over almost forehead to forehead with me trying to read it too. I smile and hand her my phone.

"Still nothing? Grrr! I was hoping there was a new baby to go see this morning." She pouts.

"There will be after three o'clock."

"That's forever to wait though." There's the pouty face again.

"We've waited seven months. What's another couple of hours?" Lifting her chin with my hand I kiss her lips. Hearing her sigh makes me smile every time.

"I know but still!"

"Are you ready to start on our own baby?"

"Why, Aaron Blake are you trying to seduce me?"

"Not really, just asking if you're ready to make a baby with me."

"I wish you were trying to seduce me and then making a baby with me." She flashes an ornery grin and turns towards the bedroom.

I smile whole heartedly and race after her. I take it we're ready to start a family of our own now. That makes me very, very happy.

***

"I'll meet you at the hospital in a few minutes Aaron. I've got a few calls to make to vendors for the Daylen wedding then I'm all yours."

"I'll meet you there then we can meet our niece or nephew. Love you."

I hang up the phone and see an email arrive in the construction account. I click on the email and am a little shocked to see it's from Payton. This lady never stops does she?

I start to read and can't seem to believe my eyes.

Aaron,

First off I want to apologize for coming out there and expecting you to want to come back here with me. I'm shocked to say that you're a changed man and it looks good on you. I'm also very sorry for treating your wife like I did. I have to admit I was a little jealous of the way you look at her and clearly love her. You and I weren't meant to be together and was pretty much an awful match from the start.

As for AB... I feel terrible for swindling you the way we did. You worked so hard to get it where it was and was the one to sacrifice what you did to get it there. Your new start in life is amazing and I have nothing but high hopes that you and Amie are happy and have the marriage and life of your dreams. She seems wonderful and I'm sure you're going to make some gorgeous babies. I know how much you have always wanted them. I wasn't willing to give you any children but I'm sure your new wife is more than willing.

Take care and good luck in your future. If you ever need anything in the professional capacity please don't hesitate to call me.

Payton

It is going to snow or maybe a hurricane's going to come our way. I hit print on the email and can't wait to show it to Aaron. Hell froze over today I think. Shaking my head and smiling I rush to the car so I get to the hospital before anything happens without me.

***

"Isn't she beautiful Aaron?" I hear Amie say from in front of me where we stand in front of the nursery glass looking at our new niece.

"Yes she's gorgeous. She looks so much like her Mama that's for sure."

"She's got Austin's hair color and nose though."

"She does. I can't wait to see what our babies are going to look like."

"Babies? Whoa tiger. I thought we were trying to make A baby? One baby."

"Well we don't have to stop there do we? There's always trying again after that one's holding its own bottle."

"That soon? You're crazy Aaron!" She smiles up at me and wraps her arms around my waist again.

"Crazy about you my love."

"One baby at a time please. We'll have ONE, and then we'll talk about another. Got it?"

"Whatever you say my dear."

"Ya'll ready to hold the newest Blake member?" Austin says from the other side of the glass wearing a blue suit and hat with the largest grin I've ever seen. "We're taking her back to Leah's room. She's all ready to meet her family."

We say yes at the same time making it impossible not to laugh at the enthusiasm. A new baby makes everyone a softy. Even Dad over here who never seems to crack under pressure has tears in his eyes as he sees Austin standing there holding his own little person.

"Let's go hold her Dad." I put my hand on his shoulder and squeeze silently letting him know I'm here and it's perfectly fine to be emotional today. He smiles and slaps me on the back before walking after Austin.

Epilogue

Two days ago- Fort Bragg, NC

"Jonathan you got a letter today. It looks like it's from a woman."
Tarley says from across the room. We got back into the US from
Iraq yesterday and they sent us here to debrief and unwind I guess.
I'd rather go home to Colvin but I'll get there as soon as they'll let
me. I can't wait to see my mom, sister and niece. She's so big
now I bet.

"Thanks man. Probably my mom or sister." I look at the envelope
and don't recognize the return address on it.

I must have a puzzled look on my face because Tarley walks over
and asks, "Too many women to keep straight?"

"Very funny. I've never heard of Temple, North Carolina let alone
been there. Have you?"

"Nope. But I'm from San Diego so I wouldn't have a clue." He
shrugs and walks out of the room.

Tarley has been my bunk mate pretty much all the way through this re-enlistment. Everywhere I've gone, he's gone too. Which is a good thing since we can't see our families for so long. It's good to have someone constant even if they're a crude person like Tarley.

I open the letter flap slowly not real sure what I'm going to find inside. As I lift the folded piece of paper out of the inside a small picture falls out onto the bed. I first pick up the picture and look closely at the little girl in it. I still haven't a clue who this letter is from and more importantly who the little girl is.

Opening the letter I see handwriting that is pretty feminine but not too legible. It's written in bright green ink and a little hard to concentrate on against the stark white paper it's written on. I squint to try and read.

> *Jon,*
>
> *So sorry to have to tell you like this but if you're reading this letter then something has happened to me. Not sure if you'll remember me or not but we met the night before you left to go back to Iraq after visiting your father's grave. You had a layover in Charlotte and we met in that dive bar by the airport.*
>
> *You were nursing a broken heart from missing your dad's funeral and I was nursing a broken heart from losing my mother to cancer that day. We drank a lot of beer that night and ended up at my apartment where we let things go way too far. You left that next morning before I woke up so I couldn't tell you I was sorry for letting things go that far.*
>
> *I knew you were going back to Iraq and wouldn't be home for a long while so when I found out I was pregnant I didn't want to burden you while you were out there fighting for our country. And I really had no idea how to get ahold of you or where you actually lived when you weren't deployed.*

I found it easier for the situation to just raise the baby alone but I continued to search for you with no luck. You're one hard man to find without knowing what your last name was. I finally ended up hiring a private investigator that found you but was instructed to only give your name and address out if something happened to me.

As you can tell by the picture enclosed you can see that we have a beautiful dark haired little girl. Her name is Arianna Elizabeth. She was born in Charlotte but we live in a small suburb called Temple. We have a good life and didn't want to intrude on yours or expect too much from you. As far as I knew you could have been married or not even made it back from your tour in Iraq.

I was diagnosed with Leukemia six months into my pregnancy with Arianna therefore I'm not sure how long I'll be around for her. Please know that I love our little girl more than life itself and chose not to undergo treatment until after I had her which the doctors say was too late. I'm doing every type of treatment we can find to ensure I'm here the longest amount of time to be with my little girl. Like I said earlier, if you're reading this letter then something has happened to me.

I'm praying that this letter makes its way to you sometime before Arianna is old enough to understand that she's parentless. My older sister Lizzie is the one whom will have custody of Arianna if something does happen to me but you're her father so she should be with you if you decide you want to be there for her. No pressure. Please don't feel you have to take care of her now, Lizzie loves her as if she were her own already so it'll be no hardship if you decide you aren't suited to be a father.

Lizzie's contact information can also be found on the back of Arianna's picture in case you do want to see her. Lizzie knows about everything and won't be surprised to get your call. Once again, you are in no way obligated to make contact with Arianna. It's up to you whether you do or not. I am very sorry to be dropping this information on you with no warning but I wanted you to know about her just in case.

Whatever you decide please know that I will be watching over our baby girl from above and love her so very much. If you do decide you want her in your life, please promise to always keep me in her life as much as you can. Don't let her forget me please. I know that's a lot to ask of a one night stand, but please think about it.

Once again I'm very sorry to drop this on you. You seemed like a wonderful and caring man during the short time we spent together and I pray you'll choose what's best for Arianna in my absence. She is the best thing to ever happen to me.

Sincerely,
Marianna Kentis

What in the world did I just read? After rereading the letter again to make sure I wasn't hallucinating, I pick up the picture of the little girl and stare at it for a long period of time. She has dark brown curls and beautiful blue eyes. She has a lot of freckles like Karlie and I can actually see a lot of Karlie in her. Oh my goodness she really is my child. Whoa I need to lie down. She's almost two years old now. I have a little girl older than my niece. Mom has another granddaughter. Holy smokes how do I tell this to my mother? She's going to kill me for this. I can hear her now, "I raised you better than that young man." Oh boy.

"So which hot mama was that letter from this time lover boy?"

"Tarley I have never gotten a love letter. Every letter has been from my little sister or my mother. Well until now." I hand him the picture of Arianna and his eyes about bug out of his head.

"Don't tell me she's yours and you didn't have a clue she existed?" Tarley says and hands the picture back. "She is gorgeous though."

With that he sits down on the bed next to me and motions for permission to read the letter. I simply nod my head and sigh back onto my pillow and close my eyes wondering if this is some crazy dream.

Nope, not a dream as I hear him say, "Holy shit man that's nuts! Do you even remember the mom?"

"Vaguely yes. There was so much beer that night and I was so upset about my Dad. Oh my goodness what have I done? I was so messed up that night waiting for the flight back to Iraq."

"Man you've got a major decision to make. Sounds like you need to make it soon too. What are you going to do?"

"I haven't a clue. I can't leave that little girl without a parent but you read it there, the aunt is like a mother so does she need a messed up Army soldier like me?"

"You're done at the end of the week so contact the aunt and meet her then make your decision. It's not too far from here and a lot closer than going to Oklahoma and back. Just because you meet her doesn't mean you have to take her home. Go and check out the place she lives and all that. Make an informed decision afterwards."

"Thank you for the advice old wise one. Nah joking aside I think you're right. I need to go and check the whole situation out. Thanks Tarley. Gonna miss your stinky ass." We bro hug it out and he leaves the room while I shower. My head is seriously about to explode and my muscles are so tense I can barely move my shoulders. A long hot shower should help. Right? Ugh.

***

"Arianna what are you doing? I told you no markers. You'll write all over the walls with those." I take the markers from her hands once more wondering where in the world these are all coming from. Marianna used to let her have free reign with them and now they're hidden in places I've yet to look.

My sister died from cancer a couple of weeks ago and I'm now the legal guardian for her almost two year old daughter Arianna. While it was horrible losing my sister, it was also comforting knowing that Arianna will always be here reminding me of the best part of Marianna. Every time I look at her beautiful baby girl I'm reminded of Marianna when she was that age.

I know a letter was sent to Arianna's biological father but I don't know what he'll decide to do once he learns of Arianna's existence. I can't help but wonder what he's like and if he'll love Arianna the way her mother and I do. I haven't heard from him yet so every day when my phone rings I get a case of the butterflies wondering if it's going to be Jon.

"I think it's time for a nap young lady. Go grab Blankie and meet me in your bedroom." Blankie was a soft pink blanket that my sister got for Arianna before she passed away. Arianna would crawl up next to Marianna in her bed and cover them both with Blankie and spend hours just talking to each other about anything and everything.

To this day she still wants Blankie and Blankie only. No blanket will do unless it's that pink one, not sure what I'm going to do when it gets worn out. I'll have a revolt on my hands when that happens.

"Ready Arianna? I'm coming you had better be lying down on that bed!" I walk around the corner and see her lying perfectly still on her side with Blankie on top of her hugging her pillow like she used to hug Marianna. That sight about made me start crying on the spot. It's the most heart wrenching thing I think I've ever seen. I wonder how long it'll be before she forgets about Marianna but I pray she never does. We talk about her Mama all the time but she knows she's in Heaven now watching over us from above. Arianna says she's her angel now and I'm okay with that because it's the truth. Marianna was an angel when she was alive so it's only fitting that she be one after death. Especially to her little girl.

"I love you Arianna. Sleep well and sweet dreams." I kiss her forehead and turn off the light while closing her door behind me.

I put my hand over my heart and let the emotions flow. That little girl is the only family I have left and if her father comes to take her with him then I'll be completely alone. That thought makes me sob even harder and I decide a long hot shower should help ease some of the tension in my shoulders.

After the shower I'm feeling quite a bit better and decide I need to get some work done. I'm an artist and have been doing paintings for the rich people of Charlotte for about two years now. I love to paint and they love my work so it's definitely a win-win. I'm also able to spend as much time as needed with Arianna and not have to send her to daycare.

I have a list a mile long of clients that want pieces painted for them but have had to put them off the past couple of months with Marianna becoming so ill and knowing she were going to pass away.

Once the treatments stopped working last year she was taking every natural remedy or special herb she could find that was rumored to help the symptoms. I took her to doctors and specialists all over the country until she came to terms with knowing there wasn't anything else that could be done to extend her life. That's when she hired the P.I. to find Jon and get her affairs in order for Arianna.

I shake my head and sigh knowing I have got to stop thinking about all of this depressing stuff and focus on the next painting that needs to be done. Just as I get black paint loaded onto my brush and touch the canvas my phone starts to beep. Great who could that be? I put the paintbrush down and lean over to reach my phone. Once I see the unknown number on the screen I instantly feel weak and sick to my stomach. This could be Arianna's dad and he could want to take her away from me.

I can't answer the beeping phone but when I hit answer on the screen it goes to voicemail. I breathe in deep and hit play on the message that's blinking.

***

"Hi um my name is Jonathan Doone and I just um, got a letter from Marianna Kentis which gave me this number to call. Um, could you please give me a call back as soon as you can? Um, I'm stationed on Fort Bragg for two more days so please call me before I head back home. Um, this is so strange. Um, I really don't know what to say here so please just call me back. Um, thank you again my name is Jonathan Doone."

I drop my phone on the floor and fall to my knees. It's him. It's Arianna's dad. He just got the letter and wants to take her away from me! He's leaving in two days and I'll never see her again. Oh my goodness this can't be happening.

I instantly dial Arianna's attorney and pray she's able to take my call. Even telling the secretary it's urgent might not get me through.

"Lizzie how nice to hear from you. How are you and Arianna doing? Things getting easier?" I hear Sylvia the attorney say before long.

"Things are. Or were. I just had a missed call and voicemail from him."

"Oh wow we knew this could happen Lizzie. Marianna only gave you custody if he didn't want to be in the picture. What exactly did he say?"

"Just that he was at Fort Bragg for two more days and then going home and I needed to call him."

"And did you call him?"

"No I called you first. What do I say and what do I do if he wants to take Arianna away from me?"

"Marianna said Jon wasn't that type of a man so we just have to pray that she was right. Give him a call back and see where he wants to go from here. He may just be in shock and want to make sure this is all real. To make sure Arianna is real. He didn't know she even existed until today. Just breathe and relax. No need to panic until you have to. Give me a call if there's anything I can do to help."

"Thanks Sylvia. I'll call him right now."

I breathe in deep and let it out slowly praying for my nerves to go with it but no such luck. I hit redial on my cell phone and hold my breath praying he doesn't pick up.

"Hello? Lizzie is that you?" Oh shit he answered. And his voice sounds so sexy. Shut up Lizzie don't be stupid. This man could take Arianna far away from you don't get all dumb and hormonal.

"Um, yes its Lizzie Kentis. Is this Jon?"

"Well yes but I don't actually go by Jon. It's Jonathan actually. Not sure why your sister called me Jon. Well, that's irrelevant actually. I'm sorry to hear about her death. That's terrible and she was so young. Very tragic."

"Thank you. Why are you calling me?" I blurt out and immediately regret it when I hear his gasp on the other end of the line.

"I'm not really sure. I got a letter yesterday from a woman I barely know and she says she was dying and that I have a little girl that's almost two years old. I'm not really sure what I'm supposed to say or do right now."

"I'm sorry that was insensitive of me. You're probably in shock?"

"Very much so. I just got back to Bragg from Iraq earlier this week and then I got the letter and picture. Please forgive me if I'm not on top of this. I honestly had no idea she got pregnant. Let alone that she was sick."

"It's okay I know the whole story. You should be pissed because you didn't know all along about Arianna. I would totally understand if you were."

"Pissed isn't the feeling I have actually its shock. And guilt because I wasn't there and I probably didn't even give her my whole name. Hell I obviously didn't even give her the correct one."

"You shouldn't feel guilty. From what Marianna told me you both were in a state of grief and being together helped to ease that pain for the time being. As a result you created a beautiful little girl."

"She is gorgeous. I see so much of my sister in her."

"And I see so much of my sister in her too. How funny is that?"

"I've only seen the picture that I was given with the letter but from that I can tell she's quite the beauty."

"I'm sorry you had to find out that way."

"Can I see her? Could I meet you? Could I see where she lives?"

"Um, yes sure. You said you're at Bragg right? We live outside of Charlotte."

"I can meet you at a restaurant first or a park. A park might be better?"

"Yes, I'll text you directions to Arianna's favorite park and then you can meet us there day after tomorrow when you're released?"

215

"You got all of that from my message? I didn't realize I told you that much. I must have rambled on. I'm sorry."

"Its okay don't worry about it. I'm just as nervous about this as you are. I love her like she was my own daughter."

"The letter said that much. Let's just meet and see how it goes from there. One day at a time. One step at a time. Sound good?"

"Perfect. See you soon Jonathan." I hang up the phone and not sure how I feel right now. Something about him made me feel comforted and not as worried. He sounded very on edge and uncomfortable. I'm not sure what else to do so I call the attorney back hoping she'll be able to help me feel better about this meeting.

"Sylvia I talked to him and he wants to meet day after tomorrow when he's released from Fort Bragg. He just got back from Iraq a couple of days ago and just now got Marianna's letter."

"That sounds like a good starting point. Just remember that he can't just take her on a whim. He'll have to prove that he's her father first and that could take a week or so. Like I said, he may just want to see her and when he sees how well you provide for her and how happy she is with you then maybe he'll bow out and leave you alone. You need to really think about if that's what you want or if you want him to be there for Arianna. What's best for her is the main goal here."

"I know. I just can't believe he wants to meet this soon. What am I saying? We've had almost two years with her and knowing he called as soon as he heard about her does say something about his character right?"

"Yes it sure does. I've seen the background check and all the information the P.I. found on him and I can honestly say he looks harmless. He came from a good home in a small town in Oklahoma."

"You've known about him for how long?"

"Just since your sister hired the P.I."

"Interesting. Well I think I hear Arianna waking up from her nap. I'll let you know how the meeting goes. Cross your fingers that he's a good guy."

"Fingers and toes all crossed." I smile at that line because that's something Marianna used to say when she was little.

"Thanks Sylvia. Goodbye." Hanging up the phone and slipping it into my back pocket I walk towards Arianna's room but stop as I get hit with a huge feeling that makes the hair on my arms stand straight up.

"Okay sis don't push. I'll meet him but don't expect much more." I smile knowing that she probably was there hugging me trying to let me know it was all going to be just fine. I sigh deep and walk into Arianna's room where she has once again found markers and colored all over the wall next to her bed. Oh goodness.

"Arianna what have you done you little turkey?" I take the markers out of her hand and have a hard time staying mad when she looks at me with those beautiful eyes and hugs me. This little girl knows just how to get her way and how to get out of a jam. I wonder where she gets that from? Yes sis I know she got it from me. I smile and go to the bathroom and get a wet cloth to clean off the marker. This little stinker and those darn markers.

***

"What did she say man? Come on spill it. You can't leave me hanging." Tarley says after I hang up the phone from talking to Lizzie.

"Dude that was the strangest phone call I've ever had to make."

"You're meeting her I hear?"

"Yes, day after tomorrow in Temple at a park. She said she would text me the directions. This is so weird."

"Did she sound hot?"

"Creep. I don't know if she did or not I was worrying about not saying something stupid." Actually she did sound hot and very kind. This could be an interesting meeting.

"You're such a liar. I'll have to go with you to scope her out and make sure she's up to par."

"Not happening. I'll let ya know how it goes though. What if she hates me and the little girl hates me too?"

"You're her dad I doubt she could hate you."

"Holy smokes I'm a dad...."

"You need to let your family know too ya know."

"I do but I think I need to meet her first and decide what to do after that. Once I decide then I'll talk to my mom and sister. I'm not looking forward to that conversation."

"Hey man do you even know for sure she's your kid?"

"Just looking at her picture tells me yes. She looks a lot like my sister when she was little. Except the hair color."

"Is your sister hot? I don't remember seeing a pic of her."

"Dude she is married and has a little girl. Go find your own hot woman good grief. Any woman associated with me and my life is off limits to you."

"You're supposed to have my back man."

"I do but not when it comes to my family."

"Family, so this little girl and her aunt are your family? Moving fast into the deep water man."

"Yes I know but there was something about the way she talked about her sister and Arianna. She sounded kind and loving. That's what all little kids need. Oh my goodness I can't think about this anymore right now. Let's go get some grub and a beer."

"Beer is what got you into this mess my man."

"Whose side are you on dude?"

Laughter is all I can hear as Tarley walks away to get in the pickup. Food and good company not revolving around a dark haired little girl is exactly what I need.

If only it were that easy. Wow I'm a dad. Me of all people. Crazy. I'm going to meet my little girl day after tomorrow and that seems so unreal.

Made in the USA
Middletown, DE
03 December 2024